MW00487645

XIII

DENYING DEATH

GARY W. CONNER, SETH LINDBERG, & BRETT SAVORY

HOUSE OF DOMINION
Canton, Ohio

DENYING DEATH

Published in the United States by **House of Dominion**
P.O. Box 36503, Canton, OH 44735
www.primebooks.net

ISBN: 1-930997-33-7

CONTENTS

DEDICATIONS

Brett

Chris Hamlin (1973-1999)

Seth

To my parents, Sandra and Dennis Lindberg, and my sisters, Melissa and Amy.

ACKNOWLEDGMENTS

Seth

Seth would like to thank Erin Heinemeyer, Amy Kalson, and Raphael Pepi for their comments on early drafts of stories and continuing support. He would also like to thank the staff of Gothic.net, Michael Schatz and Allegra Lundyworf for their interests, Alan Beatts, the staff of Borderlands Books, and all his friends that had to suffer through him whining about writers' block, and finally Jen Connolly for being who she is.

Brett

Deftones for the title and accompanying inlay image of their song "Anniversary of an Uninteresting Event" (from their self-titled album), which inspired the story within.

Mum and dad for their support of my writing.

Don Vaughan just for being the best step-dad a fella could ask for.

Sandra Kasturi for being my monkey.

CLOCKS WITHOUT NUMBERS, THE CORPSES ON THE MANTLE, AND DENYING DEATH

Michael Marano

I was watching a BBC America newscast. As I recall, one of the stories had been about "baby boxes"—things like the drawers at drive-through banks into which people dying of AIDS in African countries can place their kids with orphanages after hours—sort of the same way a North American would place a late night DVD return. An ad came on for a product that was an idol of the hubristic denial of death that makes modern living rooms places where no one can really live.

The gewgaw being shilled was a clock with no numbers.

In lieu of numerals were twelve slots into which, the commercial's off-screen pitch-man helpfully informed us, "You can place snapshots of your precious loved ones!" Think about it. Only a fairly sick society could create such a thing, and that sickness is grounded in a psychotic denial of death, a need to erase it from mental reality. I'm reminded of the group of rabbits in *Watership Down* who could never think or speak of any rabbit not present, because their apparently happy warren was surrounded by hunters' traps, and any member of the colony not in plain sight might be caught in a snare. Death is a fact of life. It's part of life. Doesn't a clock with a face that holds the faces of those you love presume immortality for them and for you? Immortality for the sense of security and stability your loved ones inspire? How could you bear to look at such a clock if one of your loved ones died, and his or her face grinned at you, frozen and reified, as the hands of the clock passed over the dead person's picture? Time *already* holds hostage all that you love, without you having to make iconography of that fact (intentionally or not). Medieval clocks, with their dancing skeletons and Reapers reminding you life is finite, seem far more sane in comparison.

If you're holding this book (Hell . . . if you've even heard of this book or any of the writers herein), you're a lover of horror. With this in mind, I want to bring up something Walter Benjamin wrote in his *One Way Street* back in 1928. Benjamin (the patron saint of intellectual slackers) argued that the origin of the bourgeois living room and the origin of the modern horror/thriller are inter-twined—think of the settings of mayhem used by Poe, Baudelaire, Leroux and Conan Doyle. (By the way, I'm aware of the irony that I, a bourgeois writer, am picking apart the Bourgeoisie; I claim my middle-class birthright to gripe about middle-class conventions.) Razor-wielding apes and speckled bands swollen with poison only resonate in a certain kind of setting. I remember a comment made by a director who staged a version of *King Lear* starring Peter Ustinov set in the late 19th century, about how all those candles, oil lamps, cigars and fashions of the time were suffocating. Maybe this is why the opulent look of those old Hammer movies is still effective after all these years. Benjamin wrote: "The bourgeois interior . . . fittingly only houses the corpse . . . The soulless luxury of the furnishings becomes true comfort only in the presence of a dead body."

It's that "true comfort" and "corpse" business as it shows up today that bugs me. A lot of us create that comfort in our living rooms by making temporary corpses of those we love in the form of those mantelpiece photos taken against bland limbo-colored backdrops, with the subjects as they would be while lying in state. The textures of those photographic backdrops are like the clouds Romantic painters used to represent cherub-choked visions of Heaven. Creepy. These portraits are a kind of emulsion-based embalming or glass-framed open casket; they preserve representations of people not how they lived, but how they'd look as one-shot characters on *Six Feet Under.*

Do you want to think of your kid forever as he or she looks with plastered-down hair and scratchy clothes as framed by an underpaid guy at Sears? Why not put a snap on the mantle of the kid in a Mighty Mouse T-shirt with chocolate ice cream stains? That celebrates how the kid *lives.* Why "pretty up" grandma so she can be parked before a scrim the color of glaucoma, when doing so rejects preserving all the time she spent in the kitchen making Sunday dinners? Why pose Dad in a suit in some overstuffed captain's chair he'd never buy for himself, when he seems happiest drinking a beer after mowing the lawn?

We don't display pictures of how we live, as if we're ashamed of them. If such pictures exist, they're hidden in dusty albums or shoe-boxes in the hall closet. Maybe it's because those pictures, by capturing life, remind us of the fragility of life. Posed portraits aren't fragile. They present the illusion that the living, extracted from life, are durable and unchanging.Formaldehyde with a flash. It's the same denial of death embodied by that kitschy clock. To those you love from the flow of life—even if it means dulling the qualities of that life by amber-trapping them in the artificiality of a photographer's studio—is to try in vain to remove them from where the flow of that life ultimately leads. "True comfort" in the living room is found in the displayed two dimensional "corpse" of someone still breathing.

I'm harping on the family and loved ones and living rooms and personal space and the home here because a good many of the stories by Brett, Seth and Gary in this book touch on those themes. *"Touch on"* might be too weak a term, come to think of it. *"Reach into"* is better. *"Probe the way a surgeon does for a lump"* is better still. A lot of these stories *hurt.* They hurt real bad. This is not a bad thing. Hurt can affirm life, and remind us we're not alone. "Empathy" is a kind of reaching into; it's as much a trespass as is the surgeon's knife, but it can be welcome. Have you ever encountered someone who is grieving, and not known it? A casual "How are you doing?" can lead to a profession of loss, the hurt of which travels along your gazes, and for the instant of that shared hurt, you're both not alone. The shitty solipsism the modern world instills in even the best of us is ripped away. The way to alleviate hurt is to share it, and the most potent way to do this is to acknowledge death with another person. The intensity of that hurt is part of life. To deny death is to numb such pain, and ultimately to deny life. These stories about the denial of death, in their capacity to hurt, acknowledge death, and in so doing embrace life in all its imperfect, messy, and at times very dark, glory.Allow these stories to hurt. Embrace that you're not alone. Time doesn't care what or whom you treasure, and if you deny the denial of death, you can treasure all the more the time you are allowed with them.

FATALE

Seth Lindberg

My first mistake was knocking: the Samoan just opened the door and shot me point-blank in the chest. I stared down at the wound in shock, as all the clever little remarks I had thought to say drifted out of my mind.

I stood there like an idiot for a second, staring at him. I thought only briefly of Laura. I took a step, it hurt like hell. I took another step. Pain: it's stupid, really. Pointless.

I put my hand around the grip of my .45 and smiled. Before, my palms were always sweaty; now they were dry as paper.

I had a mad thought he might lift his gun and do something to my face. We couldn't have that, so I fired right through the pocket of my trenchcoat. My favorite coat. It was ruined anyway.

He stumbled back, his mouth opening and closing like a fish. I wanted to say something cool and rugged, knock off a one-liner like in the movies, but when I tried to speak, I found the air cycling through my lungs via the holes in my chest. All that came out was this pathetic wheeze, like I was dying of emphysema or something.

About that time, the guy started bawling like a real kid. I looked at him, tried to speak, but still no dice. Damn.

He sure bled a lot.

The shot put him right down. He was all flab and the floor shook a bit when his back touched down. The gun retorted, muffled but still loud as all hell. *Cops,* I thought absently.

I walked over to his body. He breathed, still. I took a moment to look into the eyes of the man who had murdered me, three days ago. They weren't the eyes of anyone special. Just normal, dull brown eyes framed by skin slightly wrinkled. A vague expression of fear, and something else too, but what was hard to say.

I made a face. His eyes possessed nothing I needed to have.

I took the heel of my wingtip shoe and pressed it against his throat. Looking down at my good shoes and at his face, I saw him looking calm, and thought to myself, *He's accepting this.* It took only a subtle shift of my weight to crush his windpipe. His body struggled, but his eyes betrayed nothing.

In moments the heart of the Samoan had stopped. It seemed easier for him, somehow. The thought made me a little bitter, but I knew now that my task had ended, and I, as well, would have a chance to rest.

But I felt no grand change.

I blinked. It hurt: no tears to moisten my eyelids. The lids scratched along my eye and stung in an annoying, uncomfortable way. I didn't need to blink, but I seemed to keep doing it. Habit, I guess. Stupid habits.

I looked up and breathed an obscenity. I kept this perverse thought running through my head: all the neighbors running out and profusely thanking me for getting rid of this horrid man, and what a royal pain in the ass he was and all that crap. I knew it was stupid, I really did, but I couldn't help wanting it, or wanting something.

I guess I thought it'd all make sense. If I was going around to kill my murderer, it'd hurt like hell but I'd do it anyway just to fulfill this mad passion of mine for revenge or something.

Maybe all dead people go through this, I thought. Maybe they all just sit there and choose not to go walking around. They think, "Why bother?" They stay in their bodies, trapped in this hellish prison of a corpse, choosing not to move while the living cut them apart, fill them with formaldehyde, bury them in the cold, dark dirt.

I looked down at the cooling corpse of the Samoan, then kneeled close to him. "Get up," I said. He did not reply. "Come on," I said, pushing his flabby shoulder with my shoe. "Let's get going."

I don't know what I was thinking. Of course he didn't move. He was dead. Just dead, nothing else.

But not me. I don't know what I did wrong to be different. As far as I could tell, me and my murderer added up to more or less the same type of guy.

I walked towards the door, away from the Samoan and his entire life. I grew more and more frustrated. I stepped out, poking my head out first to see what awaited me. No one dared to leave their apartment. Good. Bored, I strode to the stairwell, the .45 in my cool, dry hand.

I walked deliberately down the steps. I felt blood sloshing around in my feet. They felt weighted down by the pressure of liquid—an awful, swollen feeling. I didn't like it one bit. There wasn't much about being dead that brought any joy to me. Soon enough I was in my car, mentally willing the damn thing to start the first time I turned the ignition key.

It did, for once, and I drove away. I didn't know how many people saw me leave that building and frankly, I didn't care. Though it would just add to the surrealism of it all if I was chased and gunned down by cops.

I drove around for a while, thinking about things. It felt like one of the bullets was still lodged in my ribcage, because I could feel something poking around there, a kind of dull, pervasive discomfort that wouldn't quit.

I contemplated getting a burger. It didn't make any sense, I know, like what they say about amputees: an itch in a limb that isn't there. It started driving me nuts, thinking about it. After an hour or so of driving around, I finally relented and pulled into a drive-through before getting back on the highway.

The burger didn't smell or taste like anything at all. In fact, it felt like eating plaster. I left it there after a few bites.

I thought for a long time, my concentration barely on the road. I thought about driving up to see my sister, or my mother, maybe visit Laura or something. But I realized how stupid that'd be. My family didn't really want to see me, and Laura and I were pretty much on the skids anyway. Nobody even knew I was dead.

I thought about how I ended up dead, trying to figure out if I missed some important clue or something that made it all make sense.

* * *

I remember him coming to me; I remember him telling me he would make it as painless as possible, 'cause he liked me so much. Because I was an average Joe like him. He just had to do it, and I understood. I had to, he had a gun in my face.

The Samoan was probably over three hundred pounds. He beat people like me up for a living. He kept going on about someone who I messed around with, to whom he apparently had some arcane connection. Probably Laura, I told myself. I couldn't think of who else it could be.

I kept telling him I didn't know what the hell he was talking about. It wasn't much of a lie: I didn't. Getting in trouble has been a way of life for me. I never hung around with a good crowd or anything and I never was the best damn guy on the planet. There must have been a mark on my forehead when I was born: something like this was bound to happen.

But the more I talked, the more he really started to rage. He wouldn't listen or even slow down and explain to me. He continued to shout while waving around this tiny gun of his, which looked so ridiculous in his huge, meaty hands. It didn't seem real; it didn't seem violent at all. I kept thinking he'd close his hand and crush the thing.

I didn't want to die and all, but he kept dragging it out and it really started to get on my nerves. It's like when you get hurt, and you know it's going to stop hurting in a bit but it's just taking forever about it. You just sit there, trying to think of good things or girls and waiting around for it to go away so you can get on with your life.

I kept waiting for the damn "whole life flashing before your eyes" thing I've heard about, but it didn't happen. Kind of crushing, really. It would have been neat.

So he went to kill me, but by then he'd changed his mind because I'm such a bastard about it all. So it had to hurt. He put these gigantic hands around my neck and squeezed. My thoughts lost cohesion and I felt completely keyed up. Kind of like having sex but painful as hell. I felt like a ragdoll in his arms, but also like a balloon under pressure, about to burst.

I could feel my tongue in this awkward position in my mouth, and started for some reason imagining how foolish I looked with this red face and goggled-out eyes. I looked back at my murderer and he had this set, concentrating look on his face like he had to take this incredible dump. And so I'm being strangled to death, and all I can think is, *Aren't we a pair?*

I must have smiled or something because he got this offended look, like I was upsetting his sense of craftsmanship in some way. I tried to breathe and failed, then I felt this pop but didn't *hear* it, and went limp.

He dropped me, muttering to himself, and left me on the side of the road. I fell to the ground with my eyes wide open. I hurt like I've never hurt before, especially my neck. I kind of knew that I had bought the farm, but still felt shocked about it all. I spent this big moment waiting for the light or for some dead relative to tell me what a happy place I'm going to, but nothing. I just sat there helplessly on the wet earth and watched the Samoan get into this tiny red Honda CRX and drive off like a nutball.

* * *

My thoughts rolled around in my head as I drove. At some point, I doubled back towards the city without even thinking. I wondered idly if I was going to start rotting any time soon. I looked at my hands as I drove: I used to chew on my fingernails when I was alive. I've been told that fingernails would still grow now that I was dead, but would I still want to chew them off? The question irritated me. Then I realized how lucky I was. I wasn't even shot in the face. The thought made me grin.

About the fourth time I drove past Laura's building, I decided to check up on her. I had nothing better to do. Her darkened flat made me think no one was home, or she'd turned in early. Somehow I doubted she had.

I parked illegally. I could.

I walked across the street, through the fog and the drizzle towards her building. The streetlights cast a strange orange glow that made the whole place seem like a dream. As I walked through the mist, it covered my face and clothing with tiny droplets of water. The whole effect was somewhat disturbing, though it made me calmer than before. As if I walked through a gateway to another world.

No one answered the bell, so I took out the key I'd made. She lived on the top floor, in one of those gorgeous apartment buildings that seem to be everywhere in this city. I walked into her flat, but didn't turn on the lights. I negotiated around a chair and a pile of laundry, looking the place over for any signs of life.

I smiled slightly. What a dump. When I'd dated her, she'd always had the place clean before I showed up, like she didn't want me to see it in its natural state. One of those girls that goes to bed with makeup on, everything she touches shrouded or masked in an order that things don't need to have.

She didn't know I had a copy of her key, but I'm like that. I always take a few precautions when I start getting to know someone. I walked into the living room and slipped off my trenchcoat. It hit the hardwood floor with a kind of *thunk.* I stopped and looked at it, then kneeled down to take out my gun.

I stood around like an idiot for a while. I really had no idea what I was going to do at her place, or how this helped me in any way. The whole thing started to get me agitated, so I decided to sit down and think about things for a while.

I slumped into a chair looking out the bay window in the front room. The mist still fell slowly, past the streetlights and the neon crucifix from the church across the street. The chair used to feel comfortable for me, but not in this state. It didn't matter; the familiarity of the chair was comfort enough. The blood in my feet and legs continued to suffer through me, and I had a casual thought about letting it out in the tub or something. Nah. Too much of a hassle.

* * *

I sat there for what seemed like forever. The mist never gave up; the darkness stayed there, not enshrouding me nor hiding anything. Just this absence of light, nothing more.

It felt better when I didn't move, if I could help it. In fact, the more limp I got, the more comfortable I started feeling.

I thought of Laura, and why I'd bothered dating her longer than any of the others. I tend to throw girls away, to tell you the truth. She didn't seem to be any different from the others. She cried as much as any of them. Everything she did showed how horribly self-obsessed she could be, and every goddamned tragedy in the world had to do with her in some way or another. It got annoying, her crying about how miserable she could be if she actually thought about things.

It was all just a game for her, though. The tears, everything. Maybe that's what I liked: the challenge of it all. I don't know. I freely admit to having hang-ups.

I hated her for being calculating, but I loved her for being so smart. I liked fighting with her, setting her off. I liked what she could be goaded into saying when she got vicious and angry. I liked it when she hit me, and I liked it when I hit her back.

I never said I was a good man.

I don't cry about my childhood like some people do. Some people just come out this way. It's not anyone's fault, it just happens.

I stopped thinking so damn hard when I heard someone

fiddling with the door. I thought I should do something, but I really didn't feel like getting up. I heard two different voices, one female, the other male. When the door opened, the woman said, "It's not much of a place, but it's mine." She sounded intoxicated.

They staggered around a bit in the hallway, and I heard the two muttering conspiratorially. The girl giggled, an unusual sound. Weird hearing Laura's voice with the tone something you can't imagine her having for the life of you.

Her alien behavior struck me. If that man were me, she would have been cold, faintly flirtatious. The whole place would have looked all set up, and we would have come into the front room. I would have sat down in this chair and we'd stare at each other's icy smiles, trading witty barbs until the bourbon finally kicked in, then we'd mess up the upholstery of her couch. I wanted to pinch my face up to show my annoyance, but didn't bother.

The man called out, "It smells like something died in here," with this nasally voice, like his tongue was too large for his mouth. The girl with Laura's voice acted conciliatory, and I heard her worrying a bit before staggering into the front room.

I had no idea what was going to happen now. But she just stood at the doorway. If she took two steps in, she might spot me in her chair. Maybe she already did. I didn't move, not a muscle.

In my lap, the .45 gleamed from the reflection of the streetlamps.

I heard her answer the guy, sounding like the Laura I knew for only a second. Then muffled noises of them talking. Fifteen minutes later I heard them having sex.

It just seemed to go on and on, pointlessly. Something so primitive and mechanical about it. I didn't know what to do, so I just sat there feeling somewhat at peace because I didn't need to move. I heard the buildup, her climax, and this weird "ugh" sound the guy made.

All right, I thought blandly. *My turn.*

I stood up, but I didn't really know even then what to do. I walked quietly to the door, where I stood for a while.

I heard her man get up and go to the bathroom. I caught a

fleeting glimpse of him, naked. The light cast him gray and yellow, and his flesh hung from his skeletal frame. As if he were already dead.

I heard him step into the bathroom. He left the door open. Good.

I walked into the hall, listening to him taking a leak. My foot stepped on a squeaky board, and I thought out a curse or two. I heard him call out, "Laura?" and her muffled reply.

I became all action. Quickly, I pushed open the door. He turned around to face me, naked and still urinating. Faster than anything, I put the gun to his face. "Don't scream," I said, flatly.

He stood there, partly silhouetted by the bathroom light, with my gun in his face. He took a deep breath.

"Don't do anything stupid," I said quietly.

I grabbed the back of his neck as if picking up a naughty cat. The flesh of the living felt indescribably hot. I just barely felt the rushing of blood under his skin. He gasped, and started to say something.

"Don't talk," I said. I pushed his head down the toilet and held it there. After a while, he stopped struggling. A little while later, the blood stopped flowing under his skin. I left him there and walked out.

I heard Laura call out his name. I turned to face her.

She stood in the bedroom doorway in one of those silky robes she liked so much, her hand gripping a sleek black automatic. The gun looked like a dagger made out of tempered black steel. All utilitarian. Beautiful, but no beauty for its own sake. Small, passionless, and deadly.

When she saw me, she gasped. I showed her my gun, and she lifted hers. "Drop it," she breathed.

I laughed. "Shoot me all you want, if it'll make you happy."

She looked at me, then at the doorway to the bathroom. "Did you kill him?" she asked.

I shrugged, which felt weird.

"Why are you here? I said I didn't want to see you again."

I told her I didn't know why. It was the truth, sort of.

We both stood there for a minute, saying nothing. After a while, she said, "You look like hell. What happened to your neck?"

"Laura," I said. "I'm dead."

She got this dumb and weird expression on her face like she didn't know what to do so she might as well cry. I continued. "The fat man strangled me." I took a step towards her, and opened my shirt. "He shot me when I came back to kill him for it."

She didn't take that too well. Fell right to the floor, her gun clattering away. I maneuvered her to the bed, then rose, standing there. The room was hot and moist with the smell of human sweat.

* * *

Time passed like it had better things to do. I just stood there. I knew she woke up and was pretending to sleep for a while, so I just sat there. The dead can be patient when they need to.

When she finally gave up, she rose and put her expression back to the Laura I knew. She opened her mouth to say something, then thought better of it. We sat there in silence.

Finally, I blurted out, "Why did you have me killed?"

She didn't say anything either way, trying to rouse this morally shocked and outraged look but not really succeeding.

After a second, she said, "You're going to kill me either way, aren't you?"

I shrugged. I didn't really know.

She started looking pretty pathetic. Put on her helpless face like it was makeup. "Why do you need to do this?" she asked. "Are you really some cold, heartless monster?"

"No, not cold," I said slowly. "Just room temperature."

She got this dark look, her eyes looking all doll-like. "I did it," she breathed. Her eyes read defiance, resignation. But behind that, an expression I couldn't make heads nor tails of.

Her voice wavered as I looked at her, but she continued. "I had the Samoan take care of you. I didn't think he'd be so messy about it."

She made a face. "I told him to be quick about it," she said. "Try not to hurt you. But you really look like hell, absolute hell."

She got a look like a petulant child. I asked her why, but I didn't really care. I'd been pretty rough with her in the past. Probably a smart thing to do for her. You can never tell with a guy like me.

Pause. "You got too close to me," she said. Probably lying. "I started falling for you, and I couldn't have that. I don't want to lose control, not anymore." She looked up, her eyes wet.

I just looked at her. She sniffed and let a tear fall. I tried to mull over what she was saying, figure out if it was the truth or not, but I kept having these perverse thoughts about making her cry harder so I could reach out and put those tears in my eyes. Maybe blink. Maybe feel human for a moment.

"I'm sorry," she whispered.

"No, it's all right," I said, matter-of-factly. Even if her answer was the truth, it didn't matter. All the order we impose on this world, it's all crap. Nothing happens for any real reason. We want to classify things; we want to have things make sense. But they don't, they never do.

But we can make each other make sense, I guessed. And I liked that, at the time.

I told her I just wanted to be dead. She put on a confused look. I told her, "I'm sick of feeling every little annoying bit go wrong. My joints are irritated. My mouth always feels dry. I have a bullet lodged in my ribcage. Everything's starting to feel stiff. It's not hell, but it's just so frustrating."

She looked at me, all sympathy. "I . . . I'm sorry. I didn't want it to happen this way."

I started to speak, but she blurted out: "I screw everything up. You deserved to die, but not like this. Every time I do something wrong it always falls to pieces."

She had this wavering look, signaling she wanted to be held, to bury her head in my chest or something. I couldn't let her, both because I felt cruel, and because I didn't want to subject her to being that close to my corpse.

I started to anyway, but then I stood up quick and held my gun out. "Laura," I said, "I'm going to have to kill you now."

"No," she said. "I can help you. I can make sure you stay dead. Let me help out; I don't want to die like this, knowing I screwed everything up."

I shook my head.

"No, really," she said, her voice raising an octave higher in pitch. "I don't want to die like this. What if you kill me and I become like you?" Her eyes went big. "I'm fragile," she said softly.

I kind of liked the idea, but doubted it'd happen. Not with my luck. "Sorry."

"Please," she said, bawling again. "I started to love you. Don't you love me?"

"Yeah," I said, surprising myself. "I guess I do." I wrinkled my brow. "Laura?" I asked.

"Yeah?" she whimpered.

"How far is heaven?"

She just looked at me. Silence for a dead moment.

I shot her in the heart. Again, the gun sounded much louder than I thought it should. The flash lit up the whole room for a brief second, like a camera, fixing that one moment forever in an image, clear as daylight.

The spent casing clattered loudly around on her lovely hardwood floor. I lowered the gun and slid it in my belt where it hung awkwardly. I half expected to fall down right where I stood. Everything came round full circle; I'd finally gone Agatha Christie. Solved my murder and brought justice to all parties involved. Everyone got what they deserved out of it.

I looked down at her, dark blood pooling around her pale body.

"Get up," I said.

I stood for a spell. Nothing happened. This wasn't about justice, or anything petty or stupid like that. I didn't know whether it was about anything at all.

I didn't wait around much before I grabbed my trenchcoat and walked out the door, into the night and neon.

The mists coalesced on my face like a woman's tears.

SILICA

Brett Alexander Savory

In loving memory of Chris Hamlin (1973–1999).
Best friends forever.

The tinkling of broken glass.

I heard it, but didn't know where it was coming from. It was like thin shards of glass being ground to dust, grating against something. Sand, maybe. Silica sand. Isn't that what glass is made from?

Silica.

It underlay every other noise I heard, as though someone was constantly sprinkling glass-dust near my ears. Faint. Insistent. On especially bad days, the suspiration of tiny glass motes became the shattering of full window panes, to the point where I couldn't see straight or even think.

In dreams, when the sound was at its dullest, my mind conjured the same image: a sliver of glass with sand flowing from its sharpest point like a runnel. Behind it and below it, only darkness, floating.

Sometimes I heard Silica's gentle breathing creeping into my subconscious as she lay beside me, dreaming her own dreams.

The combination of the sand/glass and her breathing induced in me something approaching panic, and I always woke in a sheen of sweat, my ragged breathing matching hers in time, a metronome of our dichotomous realities.

She slept so peacefully, my Silica.

I think she was the source of the sound because when she left me a few years ago it stopped. When she came back last New Year's Eve, it returned and seemed to have grown louder. I did not tell her about the glass sounds because I didn't think she would understand, and I did not want to risk losing her again.

Last week I woke up standing in front of the bedroom window that looks out at the backyard. I watched the tire-swing move gently back and forth in the soft August breeze, as the creaking sound of rope against wood fell counterpoint to the sand and glass in my head. Ever-so-faintly, beneath the creaking, the sand, and the wind, there was my love's breathing. I reached up with my left hand and put my fingers against the glass. Upon contact all sound ceased . . . except Silica's breathing. I removed my hand and the sounds returned slowly, filtering back into my head.

I looked out the window again and saw a small figure there. A child, about eight years old. I glanced over at the clock on my bedside table: 3:19 AM. Where were the child's parents? What was she doing out at this hour, alone? I returned my eyes to the figure and she looked up at me, the breeze blowing her straight brown hair about her head like something alive. She smiled softly at me, glass eyes searching mine. She mouthed one word that I couldn't make out the first time. There was too much noise for me to concentrate. I put my hand on the glass and everything stopped again, save for my wife's breathing.

The child mouthed the word again, and this time I understood it: *Daddy.*

My breath caught. The child's glass eyes glittered faintly in the meager light from the thumbnail moon. A slow, knowing smile slithered onto her face, and she kicked off with both feet in the dirt beneath the tire, swinging gently, eyes still locked to mine.

I closed my eyes, then, and thought of fire making heat, making glass, making death.

Making peace.

"Steven?"

Silica was propped up on one elbow, rubbing her eyes. "Steven, is everything alright? What are you doing over by the window, honey?"

The little girl had stopped swinging now and looked in my direction again. Not at my eyes, this time, but at my hand, where it still lay flat against the pane, keeping things quiet.

I watched that little girl die. I watched her burn to death in that house. I watched her flesh boil, watched it char in slow motion right in front of me. Her eyes bubbled and popped, running down her cheeks . . . like sand on glass.

"Steven? Hon, you're scaring me, what's wrong?"

Her screams floated through the glass, visible, living tendrils of pain, chewed up by the smoke and flames. My hand against the window, eyes holding nothing, feeling nothing, Silica pulling my other hand, pleading for me to come. The fire! Do you want to die with her? Do you!? There's nothing we can do! she screamed. They both screamed.

. . . And the child's eyes were replaced with glass.

"Steven!" Silica shook me, tried pulling me away from the window.

Again.

The child's gaze switched from my hand to my eyes, glass shards boring into my skull, cracking it, my thoughts crumbling, losing cohesion.

My little girl is dead.

"Daddy" . . .

Her voice drifted in through the open window, carrying the weight of her death, carrying the accusation.

Silica stopped pulling on me, noticing the position of my hand on the glass, following my gaze to the tire-swing that had been our daughter's favourite play spot.

"Oh, Steven, there's nothing you could have done," she whispered, wrapping her arms around me from behind, resting her head on my back. "You know that, don't you?"

Jocelyn, my sweet, dead little girl, frowned at my wife's—her mother's—words.

You could have saved me, Daddy. You could have . . .

Tears blurred my vision. I tried to speak, but I couldn't get around the lump in my throat, the pain in my heart.

Finally:

"Silica . . . let go of me."

Silica lifted her head slowly from my back, her hands fluttering as they left my body. "What did you call me, Steven?"

I ignored her. She knew her name.

"Look at her, Silica," I said quietly, tears slipping into the corners of my mouth, spreading out along my lips, salty. "So beautiful . . . and look what we did to her."

She asked again what I had called her. I don't understand why she ignored our daughter. She was right there, on the tire-swing, the way she was before she died, and all my wife could think about was her own name.

"Who is Silica, Steven?"

I felt her coldness at my back. I knew by the tone of her voice that if I turned around and looked, her arms would be crossed, her left cheek twitching a little, like it always did when she was mad. I didn't have time for that; my daughter needed me. But I wanted Silica to see.

"Honey, look at Jocelyn."

Jocelyn's face was slowly melting. My hand was hot on the glass, burning up. She screamed. She lost her grip on the tire-swing's ropes and fell over into the dirt, twitching and gurgling, skin sloughing off her bones. She twisted her head in my direction once more from her position on the ground, beetles, earwigs, and cockroaches crawling in her open mouth, her beautiful face pitted from flame and belching smoke from holes in her cheeks. Her eyes turned to sand, then, and the sound of a million sheets of glass shattering exploded in my head.

I dropped to my knees, clenching my head, my left hand sizzling against my scalp from the heat of the fire.

Silica bent to cradle me, asking what was wrong, if I was

alright, should she call 911, ohgodwhat'shappening, and still, fucking *still* asking who Silica was, all of it coming in a flood of near incoherence.

You could have saved me, Daddy. You could have . . . She pulled you away from the window, just like she pulled you away from me now, Daddy. And it happened again. Why do I have to keep dying for you?

Silica's arms were around me again; I felt their coldness, like glass, like sand . . .

After Jocelyn died, she left me. My wife left me, without a word. Every night I lay in bed and all I heard was her breathing, right beside me.

On New Year's Eve, when she returned, she brought our daughter with her . . . every night outside the window, playing in her swing, the glass in her eyes, the glass that separated me from her.

"Silica?" I whispered, the sound of shattering glass finally receding, only the gentle swish of my daughter's hair as she swung back and forth on the tire, in my mind . . . and, of course, Silica's breathing.

"I'm here, Steven," she said, rocking me mechanically under the windowsill. "I'm here."

"Silica, why didn't you let me save her?" I had never asked this question. It had never occurred to me before. "Why did you pull me away from the window? I could have saved her, Silica. Jocelyn *says* I could have. She tells me every night. But you pulled me away, you . . . pulled me . . . *from* her. . . ."

Silica was silent. Nothing. She stopped rocking me. "Why do you call me Silica, Steven?"

"That's your name," I answered, simply.

"My name is Linda, Steven. *Linda.*"

Sand slipped off the point of the sliver of glass in my mind. Silica sand. I suddenly felt very tired and I closed my eyes, thinking of Jocelyn as a baby, watching her grow up in fast-forward in my mind's eye, remembering vividly each birthday, her first words, her first steps, the way she hid under the stairs when she heard me coming, thinking every time that I didn't know where she was, then leaping out at me when I got to the bottom, screaming, "PoppaPoppaGotcha!!" and hugging me fiercely, ragged breathing in my ear from her excitement.

I remembered every time she fell from her tire-swing, cutting a knee or scraping an elbow, and always getting right back into the tire because it was her favourite thing, her favourite place.

I wondered if Silica really understood that she was gone forever.

I opened my eyes and looked up at my wife. She gazed down at me, her own eyes empty, hollow, hard, and cold.

Glass. . . .

"Silica, I'm tired. Can you help me to bed, please?"

She lifted me up and rested my top half on the bed, then swung my legs over to follow. I closed my eyes and thought again of fire making heat, making glass, making death.

Making peace.

* * *

When I heard Silica's breathing become measured, I got quietly out of bed, went downstairs, found a hammer, a handful of nails, and a packet of matches, then returned to our room, the tinkling of glass in my head getting louder with every step.

When I started pounding the nails into the wood of the window frame, Silica stirred.

"Steven? What . . . what are you doing?"

I pounded two more nails in, adding to the four or five I'd managed to do before Silica woke, and turned around to look at her. There was fear in her eyes, and I think she knew then she was going to die.

I turned from her without answer, struck a match, and lit the bottom of the window's curtains. Flames raced hungrily up the flimsy material, bathing the room in its soft, orange glow within seconds.

I walked out of the room, closed the door behind me and, using the remaining five or six nails in my hand, quickly nailed it shut like I had the window.

Silica screamed.

On my way down the stairs I heard her thumping her weight against the door, yelling for me to let her out, pounding her fists, her feet, terrified.

I dropped the hammer on the stairs, walked around to the back of the house toward the tire-swing.

As I sat down in the tire, closed my eyes, listened to the screams, and the crackling of fire, I reached up to grasp the ropes—

—and felt Jocelyn lean into me, her cheek against mine, arms around my neck, soft breath in my ear—

"Daddy," she whispered gently . . . and I opened my eyes. . . .

The bedroom window exploded outward and Silica fell, on fire and still screaming, until she hit the cobbled stone walkway three floors below, where her body shattered into myriad shards of twinkling glass.

I pushed my daughter gently from my chest and looked at her perfect face, pallid in the moonlight; her perfect long, brown hair blowing gently around her shoulders in the light breeze filtering in through the trees; her perfect eyes, no longer glass, but the deep, deep blue of the darkest waters on earth.

I closed my eyes, feeling numb, pulling my dead daughter against me and pushing off against the dirt with both feet—swinging, just . . . *swinging* . . .

I held Jocelyn tight, feeling her tears on my skin, and listened for Silica's breathing somewhere in the blanket of crackling, popping wood and roaring flame, but heard nothing.

And for the last time, I thought of fire making heat, making glass, making death.

Making peace.

THE BONEYARD ORCHID

Seth Lindberg & Gary W. Conner

Thom Wiler drove his pickup along one of the darkened lanes that wound their way through the sprawling nighttime graveyard. He kept the lights off, wary of waking the caretaker. He'd make the anniversary. He always had. The orchid sat in the passenger seat, moonlight uncovering its pale leaves.

He left the pickup parked at the bottom of the hill, then carried the orchid up towards Emily's grave. Twelve years to the day and hour that she passed from this earth. It seemed like so long ago, when they were all just kids.

He found her grave on the side of the hill, in the plot next to all of her relatives. A lot of old men and loyal wives; stark, proper stones with carved names and Freemasonic symbols. Emily's stone sat to one side, decorated plainly but strangely beautiful in its own way.

He stood for a minute, weathering the cold nighttime breeze before kneeling down to rest the potted orchid in front of the tombstone. He paused, then, trying to think of something to say. Offer a prayer or something. He'd always been awful at prayers, and he doubted Emily would appreciate them. After a moment, he rose again, folding his arms against the cold wind.

Orchids, her favorite flower. Most girls didn't even have favorites. Oh, they all thought roses were romantic in some way, but they didn't take the time to pick a favorite. Not Emily. Only orchids would do.

Bringing that kind of flower to Emily's grave felt like a completely futile gesture. Hardly anyone remembered Emily these days. They did, but not really. His old high school friends—even James or Will—got quiet when she was brought up in conversation, like they'd have put her completely out of their minds if they hadn't felt guilty about doing so. Incarceration prevented Miguel from making the trip.

So Thom came up here this year—as he did every year—to show the permanence of his memory by dropping off a flower that would die by the end of the night. And if it survived, it would only be carted off by the caretaker.

Hothouse flowers, these orchids. Emily never liked the cooler-climed deciduous orchids. Only the tropical ones would do, with strange names like 'Rynchostylis' and 'Masdevallia.' Beautiful and delicate, they die all too easily outside their protected environments.

Kind of like Emily, now that he thought about it.

Thom knew it was a futile gesture, these anniversary visits. They didn't do anything to help him cope with her death. Not even time closed those wounds. The flowers died, forgotten as she was. Life went back to normal.

He stood there, watching the grave for a while and trying to collect his thoughts, when he heard a buzzing sound. Thom froze, barely seeing the insect in the gloom of night. It was a bee; whose sting Thom was incredibly allergic to. When he was four, he had to go to the hospital from bee stings. He nearly died. His only memory of it was of an image of his sister over his bed, sobbing with helpless fury.

The bee flew around his head while Thom stood as still as he could. Finally, the bee landed on his face. Thom remained tensed, terrified. *What the hell is a bee doing out at night?* he silently asked himself. The bee crawled around his mouth while Thom remained rooted to the spot. *Maybe the flower brought it here,* he thought. *Or maybe Emily . . .*

After moments that seemed like hours, the bee flew from his face and out into the darkness.

Thom took one last lingering glance at Emily's grave and the lush flower sitting next to it, the bright colors washed out by the shadows of the night. And then he turned, and strode silently back to his truck.

* * *

He got home, collapsed on the sofa for a few moments, then went to get a beer. Walking past his answering machine, he saw the message light blinking and pressed 'play' while he cracked open his beer.

The woman's voice was pleasant and obviously recorded. "This call is from an inmate at a correctional facility. Be aware of any unlawful solicitation." There was a click, but the recording continued. The next voice was male, and he recognized it immediately. Miguel's voice still had that same charismatic cadence to it, but more than a decade's worth of incarceration hadn't toughened it. His voice wavered nervously, riding on an edge of uncertain tension.

"Thom? This is, uh, Miguel." Pause. "They're letting me out in a day or so. I was wondering if . . . well, I'm trying to get in touch with you or Will. Maybe one of you can pick me up, or maybe . . ." Another pause, long, with the sound of a sigh. "I need to talk to you, specifically, Thom. It's about Emily."

Thom hit the 'pause' button on his answering machine and frowned, looking away. He took a deep breath and hit 'play' again.

"Sometimes I think . . . maybe it's wishful thinking, I don't know. But maybe she's alive, Thom. Maybe she somehow . . . I don't know." There was the sound of Miguel's breathing. "I miss her, Thom. I see her in my dreams, every night, but I still miss her. And I keep thinking . . . something's not right about all of this. Maybe it's all the stuff that Will said, I don't know. But Thom, we have to get together and figure this out. Talk to James, I—" Miguel's voice broke there, strained with pain and anger. "I won't talk to him, but you should. See if . . . she if she . . . " He couldn't complete the sentence. He seemed to gather his wits about him, then he continued. "And Thom? One more favor? Can you bring a flower to her, for me? One of the exotic flowers, you know, the ones she liked."

Thom stared down at the answering machine as it stopped. He rewound the message and played it again, listening to the soft sounds of Miguel's voice. Thinking of orchids.

Thinking of Emily.

* * *

"I want to bleed."

It was an utterance, something that Emily said from time to time when she was feeling especially full of herself. Life sometimes got her so high that she felt that she might explode with her exuberance. It wasted no time burning her to ash.

She had been a lovely young woman, and Thom now dreamed of her dressed in a wedding gown, a vision he'd wanted to witness for far too many years before he was robbed of the opportunity.

She came toward him now, seeming to float across the floor, her bridal dress following along behind with a sighing dismissal. With each step she took, Thom felt himself being silenced, blurred, erased.

At long last she arrived before the nothing that Thom had become, and she pursed her lips as if to blow. He spent a dreadful moment praying that she would not blow away the dust he had become before she turned and walked away, a tear leaking from one eye.

As she reached the staircase, she paused and cast her head over her right shoulder to look at him one last time. "I have claimed you all."

* * *

Thom jerked awake and quickly rubbed his eyes. He pulled himself out of bed, stumbled into his waking ritual. He had too much to do today. His body had that shocked, exhausted feeling it always got when his sleep routine was interrupted.

The afternoon light angled in through the windows of his kitchen. He felt like a trespasser in his own house, stepping through the sunbeams like this. He quickly fixed himself cereal and retreated back into the darkened corners of his home.

Thom was spooning Raisin Bran into his mouth when he heard something clutter and fall down the back hallway. He paused, mid-step, then moved down the hallway. Past the closet, past the bathroom and his own bedroom, to the door that opened onto Emily's old room.

He stopped in front of the door, remaining silent. *I should call out 'Hello,'* he thought, but he didn't. He thought he could hear someone moving around in there, creeping, softly. Thom swallowed, then continued.

He grasped the handle and opened the door. Glancing back down the hallway, he stepped quickly in and looked around.

Everything seemed to be in place; even the dust didn't look any more disturbed than when he'd last been in the room. He walked gingerly to the center of the room and glanced around. "Hello?" he called out, softly.

He kneeled, to better glance into the small closet, peer under the bed. No one could be hiding here, he felt certain. He heard the sound of something settling and turned to look at the bed, intently.

He clenched his teeth. "Emily?" he called out, surprising himself with such an immediate and unlikely association.

He heard a whisper in response, and another sound. Something wet.

"Em?" he said as he rose. The lunacy of his assumption barely registered as he took a step towards the bed, the source of the sound. He threw back the blanket and found blood bubbling up from some recess within the mattress. Pooling, clotting already. And the stink, the stench of fresh gore, he could already begin to smell it.

"I don't understand," he said, not caring if the anger came through. "Why are you doing this, torturing me? *Me*? I'm the only one who takes care of you. *I'm* the one who visits you every year."

The whispers began anew, rising slightly in pitch, yet remaining just below the threshold of comprehension.

"Stop it." His own voice was at first a whisper until he gained confidence in the meaning of his plea. "Stop it! Stop it!" He left the room and slammed the door behind him.

Something cracked, behind the door. Perhaps a piece of the mirror. *Seven more years' bad luck for her,* Thom thought bitterly.

He suddenly felt utterly exhausted and turned to walk back down the hallway. He looked back and frowned.

He was greeted with the expected silence, but only at first. Then, gentle sobbing, soft as moonlight. He felt miserable, hearing the anguish behind the sobs. A part of him wished there was something he could do to comfort her . . . to *silence* her.

* * *

Thom dutifully drove back to the graveyard after a stop at a greenhouse for another orchid. He tooled around there until he found a nice, pretty, and inexpensive one. He bought it and drove to the cemetery. He carried the orchid up to join his orchid, feeling a little guilty about being cheap when it came to Miguel.

Emily already had a visitor. He wore a gray coverall, and Thom surmised that he was the caretaker. As Thom approached from behind, he could see the man scratch absentmindedly at the side of his head. He went only a few steps farther before he saw the reason for the man's apparent confusion: the orchid Thom had left the night before, a flower that Thom had fully expected to find withered and limp across the top of the gravesite, instead lilted gently in the light breeze that caressed the hilltop. "It can't be."

At the sound of Thom's voice, the man turned to face him, a quizzical look written on his sun-dried features.

Thom drew up beside him and indicated the flower. "It's not

possible. That was a *cut* flower. I put it here las—yesterday."

The man—a soiled tag ironed on the left breast of his coverall bore the name Harlan—looked back at the orchid. "Looks like someone sold you a bill of goods, son. That's a *plant.*"

Thom stepped closer to the grave, and he had to admit to himself that Harlan was right. For reasons he couldn't explain, and did not pretend to comprehend, the simple bloom that he had left the night before had somehow taken root in the earth below it, going so far as to break through the cheap plastic holder the nursery had supplied. Thom stooped to examine the thick, ropy shoots that left the bottom of the plant and grabbed at the earth.

Harlan spoke from over Thom's shoulder. "Oh, yes, this is quite a fix. Thing shouldn't be growing there, but it damned well *is*. I can't just dig it out—it's right on top of the grave, you understand. You sure you didn't *plant* this thing?"

Thom stood and turned to face him. "C'mon, man, wouldn't the ground be disturbed if I'd done that?" He glanced back at the grave. "Well, I mean, it *is*, but not like it would be if I'd gone at it with a shovel."

Harlan's chest rumbled, and then he leaned to one side and spat a wad of phlegm onto the grass near his feet. "Suppose you're right. I'm just looking for an easy answer to this one. Hell, I just mowed this area yesterday, and I know for a fact that thing wasn't here." He scratched at his cheek. "Management is gonna have my ass over this one."

"Can't you just, I dunno, *pull* it up?"

Harlan shook his head. "Nope. I did a little prodding in the soil around it—that thing's roots already extend a good four feet out away from the plant. Getting that out is gonna take some digging." He stared at the offending flower for another moment more, then shrugged. "Best be getting on down to the shop to relay the bad news." Harlan appraised Thom for just a moment. "Good day to you, son." He turned and resumed his descent.

Frustration swept over Thom, and he felt a renewed sense of panic and bewilderment. *Am I losing my mind? Has the grief that lay dormant for all these years finally consumed my sanity?* He resisted the urge to kick at the plant that now adorned the crest of Emily's grave, to fall to his knees and rip it asunder with his bare hands. Instead, he latched onto the anger that filled him, determined to use it to help him find a way out of this illogical morass that had swept into his life these last few days.

Thom looked once more at the orchid, standing tall and hale in the morning light, and he decided to find out more about this strange species that might reach into death in order to live. He reached out and snapped the nursery tag from a leafy tendril and pocketed it, frowning.

Logic seemed to dictate that Emily needed no more flowers. He carried Miguel's plant with him back to his truck.

* * *

He thought about the orchid, about Miguel, about Emily. He felt queasy, like he needed to do something. Get out of the house, figure something out. Miguel wanted him to contact James but . . . he didn't know if he could even talk to him. If they even had anything to say to each other anymore. That left Will. He hadn't talked to Will either, not for a while. Will would know what to do about the orchid. Will would verify whether nor not Thom had gone completely crazy.

He still had Will's business card in his wallet. It took him only a few moments to call.

"Hello?"

"Hey, this is Thom."

"Thom! Man, long time no talk to. How have you been?"

"I've, uh, I've felt better." Get to the point, he thought. "Will, I have a favor to ask."

"Shoot."

"Can you meet me somewhere?"

"After work, yeah. Where do you want to meet up?"

"Emily's grave."

There was a long pause on the other line. He heard Will sigh.

"Will? It's . . . it's important. I can't say why, not over the line, but . . . " How could he explain this? It seemed ridiculous, even to him. "It's just important. Just this once."

"You know I don't go up there, Thom."

"Please? Just this once?" Thom could feel a sweat sheen forming on his forehead. "I have something to show you. I promise it's real."

"Thom—"

"Please? I promise it's real."

"I'm sorry. I can't, Thom. I can't. I really wish you'd move on with your life, Thom." A quiet sigh sneaked slowly across the line before Will spoke again. "We all do. Forget about Emily, Thom. It's killing you, and there is not one single fucking thing that you can do about it—so forget it. Please."

"Will—"

Will's voice was strained. "You three were such good friends. We all were. Why did she have to get between you three?"

"Will, listen to me."

"No, *you* listen to *me*, for once. Not like any of you ever have before. You have to let go of her, you have to find some way. I know it's hard, but you have to, for my sake."

Thom rubbed his face. Will, the smaller one of the four. The quieter guy, the follower, the one who seemed happy just to chronicle the adventures of his companions. The emotional center, the one only Miguel seemed to understand. Miguel's self-deprecating cracks would bring Will out of his shell, bring that fragile smile out once again. "Will," Thom said. "I'm sorry for how I've acted, I really am."

"It's too late," Will said, sounding miserable. "It's too late for all of us."

The line went dead, but Thom listened to the phone for several more minutes before hanging up.

He walked to the hall closet for a windbreaker. As he grasped the knob, a squeaking noise caught his attention. He turned his head and watched the door to Emily's old room slowly drift open. When it finally coasted to a stop, a low keening noise emanated from the room. As it died away, the door slammed shut.

* * *

Thom stared down the hallway for a few moments, collecting his thoughts, before he brushed a hand across his hairless scalp and walked out to his battered Toyota pickup for the trip to the cemetery. He smiled as he remembered that Emily always called it the "boneyard." Emily always had her own terms for things. A woman like Emily could get away with whatever usurpation she had planned—her beauty had always been her saving grace.

Emily had once told him that, with proper care and feeding, certain species of orchid were virtually immortal. Frail and beautiful on the outside, they could be the hardiest and longest-living of Earth's many species.

Even in death, Emily's beauty would survive—so long as Thom was around.

* * *

He sat in his truck, waiting, obsessing. He couldn't fit it all together: longtime friendships were fading away, but some . . . *thing* seemed intent on filling the void. A small voice in the recesses of his mind called this thing Emily, but Thom walled off the voice, ignored it with every bit of will he could muster. He and Emily had enjoyed a unique bond in their time together on Earth, but unlike Miguel, Thom was not so foolish as to believe that even the strongest of bonds could survive the grave. He frowned, feeling sick.

He heard a car passing and glanced up, looking for Will's Subaru. Hoping he'd changed his mind.

Nothing. He looked away, again, back up to the cemetery. After two hours, he drove home.

* * *

His phone was ringing as he walked into his apartment. He ran to grab it, managing to answer before his machine picked up.

"Yeah?" he gasped.

"Thom, it's Will. Something's happened. James would have called you, but he's too messed up right now."

"What's going on?"

"Thom, Miguel is dead."

Thom felt himself fall back slightly, finding the nearest wall.

"Thom? You there?"

"Yeah, I'm here." No need to send out a search party, cause he was right there on the wall. Yeah, he was getting a little lower all the time, but this wall was a temporary best friend, one that he wouldn't mind hanging with for at least a couple hours.

"It was a—" Will paused. He could hear his friend take a breath, catch his thoughts. "A car wreck." He said the words slowly, ponderously. "He was on his way home. Fresh out of jail—I know James told you he was getting out. He was coming to see us."

Thom had reached the floor, was beginning to lose feeling in his hand. *Am I still holding the phone?*

"Thom, are you going to be all right?"

Thom gripped the phone hard to assure himself that he still had a firm hold. He had an image in his head, he and Miguel out fishing up in the mountains. He always seemed so calm, but this time he seemed nervous. *I want to ask you something,* he said, turning to him. *It's about Emily.*

What's that? Thom said, turning to him. In his memories, Miguel looked perfect, without blemish. *Is something wrong?*

No, nothing's wrong. It's . . . it's your permission I want, really . . .

He banished the memory by shutting his eyes, holding back the tears. *It's not fair,* he thought, *it's not fair. Eleven years for a crime you didn't even commit.* He could imagine the way the car would be twisted, the glass shattered, Miguel's life flowing out onto the pavement. *You won your freedom, though. You got out. But was it her that did this to you?*

"Thom, are you there?" Will's voice wavered, sounding concerned, frightened. "Are you all right?"

"Yeah . . . yeah, I'll be cool." He sucked in a heaping breath. *Was it you, Emily? Did you kill him?* "Tell me something, Will."

There was a slight pause. "What's that, Thom?"

Thom cleared his throat before continuing. He thought of those last words Miguel said to him, said to his answering machine. "Did Miguel mention any weird dreams? Maybe he saw someone who looked like Emily somewhere?"

"Miguel was in prison for the last eleven years, remember? Generally, there aren't too many women parading around a male penitentiary."

"I'm sorry, it was a stupid question." Thom glanced toward Emily's room, perhaps expecting some sort of commotion from that quarter. "Listen, Will, I really have to talk to you guys—you and James. I need you to come over here as soon as you can."

"That's probably a good idea, but I don't know if James will be up to going out just now."

"Just wait," Thom said. "Hear me out. I think Miguel was only the first. Maybe you're next, maybe James, maybe *me*. But there *will* be another, and then another. I have some things I need to tell you about—the *both* of you. Can I expect you in thirty minutes?"

There was a long pause, and Thom thought perhaps he'd blown it already, but finally Will sighed and agreed that the three of them would meet.

Thom hung up and took a seat at the kitchen table to wait. As he sat and stared out the nearby window that overlooked the field behind his house, he turned the events of the last few days over and again in his mind.

He felt like he was missing something, something important. Something that would tie it all together. But what?

He rubbed his face with his hands. *Maybe I killed him,* he thought, helplessly. *Maybe I made it look like he died. Maybe I'm not in control of my life, maybe* she *is.* In his mind's eye he saw the door to Emily's room, closed and imposing, somehow cold. *Maybe she's bringing them over to enact her revenge, take them out of the picture. Leaving only me, her caretaker, to watch over her until I die.*

Thom snapped to when there was a loud rap on the door. His eyes found a clock, and he wondered where the time had gone. He remembered that he was supposed to answer the door, and he rose to do so. When he walked into the hallway, he cast a glance at Emily's door, just to be sure that all was serene.

Satisfied, Thom reached the front entrance and drew the door back. Will stood on the doorstep, James slightly behind him, on the steps. It had started raining, and James was in the process of getting soaked.

Thom stood aside and begged the both of them in, closing the door behind James. "I'm glad you came. I wish the circumstances were better."

James offered a sullen look and made no attempt to remove his slicker. Rivulets of water cascaded across his face, escaping the tangled web of hair that genetics had gifted him with. His eyes looked like hell, bloodshot and red-rimmed. His face was pale and wan, as if he was already dead. "What the hell is this all about, Thom?"

"Just take off your jacket and make yourself comfortable. You're going to be here awhile, I think."

Will pulled back the hood of his raincoat, then wiped some water away from his face. "What's going on, Thom?"

* * *

"Do you like it?" Thom asked.

James hovered near a windowsill, looking over a small plant with thick, meaty leaves and purple flowers. "This is a violet, right?"

"Butterwort. *Pinguicola vulgaris.*"

"Oh, right. One of those special plants you like," he said, sounding disinterested.

Thom felt a stab of frustration. *Not what I like, what* she *likes,* he thought. *You thought you knew her so well, but you never knew her. You never understood her, not like I did.* "An orchid, yeah. Or related. They grow in bogs. They—"

"Are they hard to care for?" asked Will, curiously.

Thom turned to him, glancing at James. James seemed

exhausted and worn. He'd been too hard on him, he suddenly realized. Miguel's death . . . it shattered him. "They . . . no, not hard at all." He turned, looking at Will's face. His look seemed urgent, but then, perhaps he was striving hard to find something normal to talk about. "Just have the right amount of peat in the soil. You don't have to even worry about nutrients, just water it."

"Why not?" Will asked, urgently.

Thom turned to study the plant. "They get it from insects."

"You mean, it kills the insects," Will said, softly. "It gets what it needs from their bodies."

"Yes," Thom murmured, not looking at James.

A pause hung over the room, leaving only the patter of rain from outside as conversation. It continued without them, as rain always has and always will. Finally, James spoke, in a leaden voice. "Why are we here, Thom?"

Thom sighed heavily and ran a hand over his scalp, a nervous habit that had seemingly developed without his complicity. "I left a bloom from one of these plants at Emily's grave last night." He looked to James, offering something of an aside. "I do it every year. *Someone* should remember her."

James tensed, started to offer a retort, but Will quickly put it to rest. "And?"

Thom gathered a breath. "It took root. It's *growing*. On Emily's grave. Even the caretaker didn't know what to make of it. You should see it—roots as thick as my finger."

Will looked uneasy, and a shift in his posture enhanced the appearance. "Well, that's certainly strange. But, again, what's the point, here?"

Thom couldn't help but be exasperated. "Will, this kind of shit doesn't *happen*. Plants don't take root that quickly. They don't grow overnight. Don't you understand? This is serious. Something's going on."

Will gave Thom a long look. *He thinks I'm nuts*, Thom thought. *He thinks I'm making this up*. Will's gaze shifted to James, and an emotion that Thom couldn't quite read—confusion? fear?—passed briefly over his features, then something seemed to settle behind his eyes, as if he'd reached some ultimate conclusion.

"I . . . I'm gonna go grab another beer," Will mumbled. He ambled down the hall towards the kitchen. Thom watched him go. As Will passed the door to Emily's room, he stopped and visibly shivered, then gave the door a curious look before hurrying away.

Thom turned to look at James—or rather, his back. He thought of what to say, but didn't know. They had been best friends, and now this. Now everything. Now they stood alone together in a room, feeling like they inhabited different universes. *When did it happen? I forgave so much of you,* he thought.

James turned, slightly. Thom saw his fist clench, then unclench. Thom took a step back and watched James, the butterwort in his peripheral vision. A beautiful flower. A strange and terrible beauty.

"Miguel's dead," James said, flatly.

Thom swallowed. "Yeah. Will told me."

"I . . . " James looked up at the ceiling. "I didn't write him either, you know. But . . . "

"He wouldn't have wanted you to write," Thom replied, sounding cold, colder than he'd intended.

James clenched his jaw. "I know. That's why . . . " He stopped.

Thom watched James fight for words. *Is that why you're so furious at me,* he thought, *that our friendship died the day Miguel went to jail? Because I could have talked to him, and decided not to, a choice you were never allowed to make?* "Jamie," he finally said.

James turned, looked Thom in the eye. He said nothing. His eyes were a startlingly deep blue, almost violet. *It's his eyes,* he remembered Emily saying once. *It's his eyes.*

Will walked back in, twisting off the top of a bottle of beer. "What'cha guys up to?" he asked, a forced cheerfulness about him.

"Nothing," James said a bit too quickly. James gave Thom a strange look.

Thom glanced at Will. "Just reminiscing about Miguel."

Will got a sad look. "Yeah . . . " He glanced at his shoes, then looked back up. "You know what we should do? Hit the Roadhouse in Miguel's memory. He would have wanted that."

Thom hadn't been to the Roadhouse in years. But it never felt the same way since they had gone when they were kids, sneaking in to see local acts or just act beyond their age. Miguel always had a more mature look about him, he never got carded. Back in the day, the Roadhouse was an exotic locale, there held the strange and wondrous mysteries of adulthood.

Now it seemed like any old bar with cheap wood paneling, booths with holes in the seats, sticky floors, lumpy pool tables. The kind of women that went there Thom had gone to high school with. He had watched them marry their high school sweethearts, divorce them when the sweet perfect union started to show flaws. The Roadhouse was a place where charm wore off like old chrome.

"Sure," Thom said, "for Miguel's memory."

Will grinned. "Cool! We'll party so hard, we'll tear the damned place down."

"I don't know about it, guys," said James. His voice had an odd tone to it.

"Oh, come on!" said Will. "You have to."

James glanced at Thom while Will pleaded.

"Just for a while," said Thom. "Then we'll both split."

James glanced back out the window. "Okay," he said, with great resignation. "I'll go." *He looks like he knows something*, Thom suddenly realized. *But what*?

On the way to his car, Will turned and glanced back at the house. "Whoa," he said.

"What?"

"Thought I saw someone in the window for a second. Weird."

Emily. "That's nothing. A trick of the curtains," Thom lied. "Used to spook me like anything before I figured it out."

"Oh," Will said, watching the window for one long moment before sliding into the driver's seat of his Subaru. His eyes betrayed his disbelief, glancing once back at the house with a tight frown on his face. James clambered into the back and Thom squeezed into shotgun, glancing forlornly at his truck. *I should take it*, he thought. But he let Will drive. Will was the more responsible one, anyways.

* * *

"You'll never forget her!" The words were scrawled across the porcelain tile in thick but faded black ink, and a telephone number had been included just beneath it, but Thom's outstretched hand obscured the last four digits. He wobbled on his feet as he considered lifting his palm to reveal more, but then his urine began to flow and his stunted attention was drawn away and the cryptic message pressing against his flesh was forgotten.

He took a great gulp of air and relaxed his muscles, immersed in the base enjoyment of relief. He closed his eyes for just a moment, only long enough for his vision to reveal itself as starry and swimming against his eyelids, and then he forced them open and refocused his efforts on keeping his shoes dry.

The bathroom door creaked open behind him, and his stream faltered for just a moment, but he saw that it was only James and he picked up quickly where he left off, his efforts somehow redoubled for the intrusion. "What's up?" His voice, slurred by one pitcher too many, fell against the wall mere inches from his face and then bounced around the small chamber. He peered over his shoulder, his business nearly done, and saw James glance about, assessing the layout.

"Still just the one hole?"

Thom offered a short bark in the way of response, then fumbled with his zipper and stepped back to clear the way for his cohort. He stumbled to the sink and grabbed onto the lip for support. As his addled brain tried to reconcile itself with the yellowed basin and the calcified tap, he suddenly realized that James was speaking.

" . . . no idea who the chick is, but, hey, it's been a long time, you know?" James punctuated whatever it was that he'd said with an alcohol-fueled howling noise.

Thom found that he wanted to be angry, very angry in fact, but he wasn't sure why. He realized that he wasn't sure of much at all, then he tried to reestablish his bearings. He considered the sink, the faucet, decided that the single spring-loaded tap was far too much of an effort. He raised his hands before him, as if germs might be visibly present. Finding nothing that begged removal, he dismissed entirely the concept of rinsing his hands and staggered out the door.

He stood outside the restroom, taking a long moment to locate the table he and his group had occupied, and he'd no more than spotted Will when he noticed that Will was engaged in deep conversation with someone leaning on the table. It was a man, bearded, heavy, even dangerously so were one to judge merely by the sweat stains that marked his back and armpits. Thom struggled to identify him, certain that he would be easily able to do so had he not already plied himself with drink. His train of thought, however, soon went far off the rail, and his mind returned to the same well-worn synapse: Emily. Emily, death. Emily, death, orchid.

At this last word, something snapped in his head and he recalled exactly what he'd been planning to talk to Will about some two hours—and two or three pitchers—before. Fixated, he carefully negotiated his way through midnight ballerinas and eight-ball prima donnas.

As he neared their table, he called out to Will. "Parasite!" It was nothing more than a blatant and necessary reminder to himself of what he wanted to bother Will with, but both Will and the rotund gentleman leaning over him turned to look at Thom with intense expressions bordering on menace.

Thom was too drunk to let that get to him. He splayed himself on the bench in front of Will after moving carefully over. Fat stranger had moved on, and Thom spent only a moment more wondering after him, trying to discern just who the man was and how he knew him.

"Orchids," said Thom, fixing Will with a drunken gleam in his eye. "I've done quite a bit of reading on them, you know. Some orchids grow on other plants, kind of like barnacles grow on whales. They're almost like parasites."

Will's posture didn't change, but he seemed to tense, to grow somehow larger in Thom's influenced estimation. Will still leaned across the small table, nearly in Thom's face—an odd, dull look in his eyes—and yet he'd somehow become menacing without so much as flinching. His face seemed to be mere inches from Thom, and Thom thought that perhaps there was a wildness written upon it.

"What's wrong?"

Will seemed to consider this for a moment before he sat back in the booth and tried to relax—even though Thom could still read the unease in his features.

Will sighed, looked around at the motley patrons for a moment, then returned his gaze to Thom. "Nothing at all. You feeling good?"

Thom considered the myriad of possibilities such an innocuous question begged before he finally declined to answer.

"I thought this would be a good idea," said Will, solemnly. "It wasn't, was it?"

Thom frowned. "It was a great idea, Will. It's just . . . " He glanced back, to where James was. He was leaning a bit too heavily on the jukebox, paging through the selections, while making furtive glances up at a booth in the back where four women chatted with one another. Thom looked from James back to Will's sullen face. "Sometimes . . . now, don't take this the wrong way . . . "

Will's face darkened and his body seemed to tense, perhaps assuming a defensive posture. "Just say it, Thom."

"Sometimes I think you just want things the way they were. You know . . . back . . . "

"Back when the four of us were best friends."

"Yeah. But . . . there are old wounds. Bad memories. We can't go back there, not anymore."

"Thom?" Will's voice was as careful as it was strained. He stood.

"Yeah?"

"You're one to fucking talk." He shook his head, looking

flushed, and started to stalk towards the door.

Thom blinked, and headed after him. "Hey, Will. What the hell?" The bar was a loud cacophony of voices. He could hear Will muttering ahead of him but couldn't figure out what he was talking about. There was a crowd right at the front, full of people his age. The kind of people who now had husbands and wives, had fallen into a pleasant rhythm of life, were satisfied and happy. Went out on nights like these sometimes to remember what it was like to be young and dangerous again, and sometimes just to get away from it all. One of them turned and glanced at the two of them, a flash of recognition in his eyes. "Oh, hey. Thomas, right? And Will?" This guy was tall and thin, a bit of a receding hairline, a saccharine grin on his face. He had to shout a little at this end of the bar, and he shouted a little louder than he needed to.

Will glanced up, frustrated, and stopped his exit for the time being. Thom caught up and nodded to the man. "Hey." The face looked familiar, but he couldn't tell where.

"Man, I haven't seen you guys since high school." He scanned their faces, then said, "Remember me? I'm Stuart. From that shitty Life Sciences class, tenth grade? I sat behind you."

Thom could barely remember it, but the face came back. A little longer, more bony. Tangled brown hair once fell in his face; now he had a receding hairline. He used to prop his head up with one hand, stare out the window throughout class, just space out completely. He looked like those pictures of P.O.W.s in the history textbooks. Thin, tired, vacant.

"Jesus, those were some good times. Remember when James pulled that prank on Mrs. Summers?" Stuart laughed, and shook his head. "Sometimes I wish I could go back to those times." Will flushed, angrily. The man, oblivious, patted his gut. "Or at least look like I did!" He laughed again.

"Yeah," said Thom absently, glancing around for James. "High School was a long time ago."

"It sure was, it sure was," Stuart said, almost piously. He then softened, got a concerned look, staring at Thom. Thom glanced back. "Oh, and I'm sorry, I heard about your—"

He didn't finish the sentence. Will suddenly made his way for the door, pushing against the man and sending him sprawling off-balance. The bar patrons turned around to stare curiously. Will was already stalking out the door, people stumbling out of his way.

"What the fuck?" Stuart spat out, coming up and leaning forward, his stance aggressive.

Thom wanted to get to the door, get to Will and see why he was so upset. He looked back at Stuart. "I'm sorry, he's had a bit too much to drink."

Stuart sputtered out something in response, speaking with subtle shades of violence. Thom stepped back, frowning. "No need to get upset."

"What's going on here?"

Thom turned. James smiled at him, all charm and alcohol fumes.

The man turned to James and eyed him. "Your friend Will's a dick," he said flatly.

James shrugged with a casual nonchalance. "He gets that way when drunk. Stu, right?"

Stuart grinned. "Yeah, James! You still kickin' it with the ladies?"

James looked mock-offended. "Of course!" He turned to glance at Thom, raising an eyebrow just a bit. Thom read it as *what the fuck's up with Will?*

Thom shook his head, as if to say: *don't know, I'll go find out.*

James nodded, then put an arm around Stuart, guiding him to the bar.

* * *

Thom stepped fluidly out of the bar and onto the cracked asphalt of the parking lot. He quickly looked around to see Will already in the driver's seat of his Ford Focus. Thom ran over. "Hey, what're you doing?" he shouted, rapping on the window.

Will rolled it down, shooting him a look of frustration and

anger. But the fury didn't seem to be directed completely at Thom, the anger and hate seemed to be somehow self-directed. But . . .

"I need to get away from here," Will said, dully. "I need to think about a few things."

"But what about us? What're we going to do for a ride?"

Will shrugged. "You don't live too far." He glanced back out at the road, shifted into reverse, and backed out of the parking space, barely missing Thom. "You know what's wrong with you two?" he said, using the edge of his voice.

"What?" said Thom, feeling defensive himself.

"You and he," he said bitterly. "And Miguel. You took such effort to reconstruct her memory that you stopped living, almost. You've been denying life and embracing death. And it's just such a shame." There was the sadness of defeat in his voice. He put the car in gear and drove off.

Thom stood there, faintly shocked. *He'd never do something irresponsible like that. But he just did.* Thom shook his head, then glanced back at the bar. Time to go talk to James.

He felt watched. The feeling was palpable in the air; Thom could almost smell the intensity. He narrowed his eyes and scanned the parking lot.

He caught a gaze and locked in on a face that was weathered and bearded with dark, unruly hair that seemed oily, tangled, and knotted: a stylist's nightmare. An intense expression, like a cat calmly studying a rodent. The man's thick, flabby arm hung over the open window of his car. He narrowed his eyes with a thoughtful intelligence, and then turned away from Thom, pulling out of the parking lot as well. He drove in the opposite direction from Will.

There was nothing about the look that should logically have made Thom uneasy, but he was. Something about that man, and Will's association with him, set Thom on edge.

* * *

Inside, James had put Stuart enough at ease that Stuart

demanded to buy a round of drinks for them. They drank and talked for another hour, James seemingly unruffled by Will's angry disappearance. The large booth grew crowded and Thom found himself squeezed a little too close to a woman with flat brown hair and an overly-large sweater. She did her best with every trick of body language to show her lack of interest in Thom.

Maybe I wouldn't have wanted to end up with you, he thought bitterly. He looked over at James, who had some long and complicated anecdote halfway finished. The woman next to James looked like she'd give half her molars to laugh at the end of it. Her frizzy blonde hair looked tensed to shake in glee.

Even Thom ended up buying a round as the night progressed. He dragged James away after James' rather blatant and drunken proposition to the laughing woman. Anyone else probably would have been slapped, but he just looked piteous and the woman ended up looking flattered. Thom shook his head. The game made no sense to him.

They staggered out, both luckless, though Thom by choice. "Where's the car?" James said, confused.

"Will drove off in it."

He smacked his head. "Oh, tcha. Right. Well, you got your truck, right?"

Thom gave James a patient look, and didn't respond.

"You mean we have to walk?" James' voice rose up in decibel as well as pitch.

"Yep, unless you can afford a cab."

James shook his head. Glumly, he staggered down the road homewards with Thom. "Hey," he said, suddenly sounding serious. "That brunette next to you was hot. I think she wanted you."

"You know what, James?"

"What?"

"You're still full of shit."

"You just figured that out?" James grinned. He flashed Thom a gaze of dark blues. In his memory, he could hear Emily say, *It's his eyes.*

* * *

A mile or so of walking and they passed by the graveyard. Thom had forgotten it was on their way. Maybe he could find the caretaker, Harlan, and get him to drive the two back. Or maybe show the flower to James, then James would understand the gravity of the situation, or at least be a witness to just how weird it was.

He suggested they detour through.

James scrutinized the graveyard. "Didn't I see this in a horror movie?"

"Sorry, I missed *They Cut Through The Graveyard* when it was in the theatres."

"You mean you don't have it on DVD?" James shook his head, sadly.

Thom chuckled, then looked back at the dark graveyard. It didn't seem terribly scary, though at one point in his life it probably would have. But *she* was up there, and that plant on her grave . . .

"We can take the long way back. Too many white kids die already in movies doing stupid shit like that."

"You're a white kid."

"Sure, all the better reason not to go."

"So, you're denying your cultural heritage now? It's practically your *duty* to take the shortcut."

James glowered at the gates. "Bring my cultural heritage into it, why don't you." He sighed. "Okay, I'll go."

The graveyard was peaceful at night. The calm spread over the pale gravestones as they stretched out through the trees and climbed the rolling hills. Thom and James followed a flagstone path that wound through the various plots.

"Which way is her grave?" James asked.

Thom blinked. "You mean you don't know?" He tried to make his voice sound half-joking, hiding the deep annoyance he suddenly felt.

"I . . . I've never come. I couldn't."

"What do you mean, you couldn't?"

"I just couldn't." James' voice sounded hoary, at the point of cracking. "It doesn't matter," he mumbled, looking up at the tombstone-covered hill. "I have her with me every day."

Thom gave James an odd look with that. "What do you mean by that?" he asked, cautiously.

"Nothing. You wouldn't understand." James' voice grew firm.

"Maybe I would."

James didn't respond. He followed Thom up as they walked through the graves. Thom still felt a little drunk, but his mind was sober and calm. It had something to do with the mood of the place. They were lucky: a warm spring night like this usually teemed with insects—moths, mosquitoes and the like. Tonight, though, silence reigned.

"She had a word for these places," James quietly said, reverence in his voice. "She had all those funny words."

"A boneyard," Thom replied.

"Boneyard, yeah." James laughed, a laugh shrouded in pain.

From there, it was a short walk to her gravestone. When they approached, Thom thought he saw a figure standing in the shadows in front of the grave, kneeling down, possibly weeping. When he walked closer, he saw it was the flower. And oh, how it had grown.

They both stepped carefully towards it. The ground seemed dark in the shadows, like freshly unearthed dirt. The orchid twisted up towards the sky, its succulent flowers almost carnal in their appearance. James gasped.

Thom took another step forward, and his foot made a crunching sound on the grass.

"What the fuck?" James finally said.

Thom kneeled down, then felt through the grass. He felt something like thorns and feelers, and a thousand tiny sensations across his skin. Revolting. "Insects," he said.

"Alive?"

"No, dead. Corpses."

"Husks," James corrected. He moved closer, his feet crunching as it crushed the bodies of what must have been thousands of insects scattered around the flower.

Thom turned and glanced up at James. James' look was reverent. "I know this flower," James said.

"You do?" Thom asked, then looked at it. It seemed twisted and smooth, upraised to the sky, as if in prayer.

"Yeah. Emily gave me one before she—" His voice cut off.

"Before she was killed," Thom said, quietly.

James stood in silence. Even though his face was shadowed, Thom could see the glint of his tears on his face. Thom fought for something to say, but the silence lingered on.

It was finally interrupted by a crackling sound from behind them as more dead insects were crushed underfoot.

Thom rose to his feet and turned even as James swirled and stumbled backward over a marker that jutted crookedly from the soil. A flashlight robbed Thom momentarily of his night vision, and he squinted and held up a hand to diffuse the blinding ray. The beam swung quickly to James, laid out on his back and fumbling for purchase, and jumped just as quickly back to Thom, this time aimed more toward his legs.

"Some kind of anniversary?"

Thom immediately recognized the voice as that of the caretaker. He spoke as he watched James finally clamber to his feet. "Um, no sir. We were just passing by and thought we'd stop in. Why do you ask?"

The flashlight danced a bit closer before the man tucked it up under his arm in such a way that it pointed mostly skyward, yet illuminated their small group. Harlan's face appeared much older in the bad light, and Thom briefly wondered how old he himself must look on such a night where grown men gathered in graveyards and chatted in the weak glow of a few D-cell batteries. The beam wiggled and lost itself against the darkness of the sky as Harlan wrestled a cigarette from his shirt pocket and lit it. "Your lady there entertained another guest not fifteen minutes ago." He punctuated his statement by shining the flashlight on the grave before shutting it off.

Thom wanted very badly to be shocked by this revelation, but it seemed dulled by all that had come before it. The last twenty-four hours had been a blitzkrieg of too much information, and he just wasn't sure that he was at all capable of dealing with things like a rational adult—not anymore. Instead of freaking out completely, he drew a deep breath—he had never smoked, but at that moment he wanted very much to steal the old man's cigarette and draw in every bit of mild intoxication that the thing could offer—and he amazed himself by calmly questioning the man. "A visitor? Did you see who it was? Do you know him?"

In the dim light offered by Harlan's cigarette, Thom could barely read the disdain on the man's face. He spoke around his butt even as he released the last draw. "Don't know of him, no. Heavy-set fella. Sweaty. Hairy. Wasn't here long—just long enough to catch my attention, but not long enough to let me have a talk with him."

Thom immediately made the connection. He turned to James, who was wiping at the fresh grass stains on his trousers and cursing under his breath. "James, did you see that guy that Will was talking to back at The Roadhouse?"

James grunted in response and stood, apparently seeing the futility of his cleaning efforts.

"Do you know him?"

James seemed to consider this for a moment, then shook his head. "No. He seemed awfully familiar, but I just can't place him."

Thom nodded thoughtfully. "Same for me." He turned back to Harlan. "Anybody else been visiting these parts in the last couple days?"

Harlan opened his mouth to speak, but he was cut short by a voice from the darkness behind him.

"Me, of course." Will stepped into the small circle of yellow light cast by the old man's cigarette. He nodded at Thom. "Waited in your driveway for a while. When you guys didn't show, I thought you might have stopped off here."

The spinning in Thom's mind had picked up a notch at Will's sudden appearance, and it showed signs of accelerating once again. Thom hoped that he might remain standing, alert, conscious. "You've seen the orchid, I suppose."

Harlan flicked on his flashlight once again and shone it briefly on the plant, as if to punctuate Thom's query.

Will walked over to the orchid. "Yesterday. I have to admit that I didn't believe you, so I came to see it for myself. It's quite a sight, isn't it?" He ran a hand down the plant's thick stalk.

Thom could not help but cry out. "Don't touch it!"

Will turned to his friend, an odd grin stretched across his features. "Oh, I'm going to do much more than touch it. Much more." He pulled his jacket flap aside to reveal a meat cleaver tucked into his waistband. "This fucking thing is coming down. Tonight."

Before Thom could grasp this new development, could see a clear path to what had to be done next, James had already done it: he quickly leapt in front of Will and pushed him back, away from Emily's grave.

"Just wait a goddamn minute, you crazy bastard. A *meat cleaver.* Sometimes I wonder how in the fuck I ever got hooked up with either one of you idiots." He cast a glance at Emily's headstone, then fell silent.

Thom finally gathered himself and put a voice to the question that had been nagging him ever since he staggered out of the bathroom at The Roadhouse. "Will, who was that guy you were talking to at the bar? That fat guy with the beard."

"You don't know him."

The answer struck Thom as less than forthcoming, but before he could demand more James interrupted.

"Bullshit! I know that guy from somewhere."

Will grinned smugly. "You ought to—always good to be aware of the competition."

"What's that supposed to mean?" Thom's head was spinning again, and quiet voices had begun to whisper in the back of his mind, saying things he very much didn't want to hear.

. . . My darling man, my hero, my savior . . .

Thom felt tweakish, as though he were back in school and back on the meth—very little ever made sense to him in those days, and absolutely nothing seemed to make sense now. Distantly, he heard Will and James exchange angry accusations. James' voice was desperate and strained; Will's seemed edged with a steely resolve. Out of the corner of his eye, Thom saw the old caretaker start to slowly back away, his flashlight's beam dimming with the distance.

Thomas!

He took a deep breath. The air was heavy with the perfumed scent of the orchid, which strained and crawled its way towards the sky. Will and James faced off below it, and they seemed to grow perceptibly smaller even as Thom watched, as though the orchid was feeding again. "Some big fucking insects," Thom said, and a cackle nearly escaped him.

The argument intensified, and Will and James began to close on one another. I have to do something, Thom thought. I have to—

You have to save me. The voice in his head returned, calm and clear, somehow more reasonable than all else around him. *You're the one I've always been closest to. You're the one I'm truly tied to. We're bound together in ways no one else could hope to understand . . .*

"You can't just *kill* it!" James pleaded. "We don't even understand what it is yet, why it's there!"

"Understand? Understand?" Will almost roared. "That . . . *thing* there, it's a damned parasite, James! It's feeding off you guys, like it fed off of Miguel!"

And they're jealous of that, the voice plainly stated. *Jealous of that connection. Will has always been jealous, since long before I was alive. He always hated me.*

Thom stared at the ground. "I'm sorry I killed you," he whispered, barely making it out over a choking sob. He could still imagine it, going after James with the knife, Emily jumping in the way. He had relived the image in his mind a thousand times, laid awake at nights. James' face: confused, broken, shocked. And Emily's eyes growing wide as she tried to let the blood that welled inside her, as she coughed up the blood she must have been drowning in. He could never banish that image from his head. Never.

I'm sorry as well, the voice said, sounding small and terribly alone. Fragile. *For keeping that secret: the one secret I've ever kept. It wasn't right, I know that now.*

Thomas felt awash in pain and grief, all over again. He covered his face, his breathing ragged.

It's all right, she said, soothingly. *You didn't mean to. But Will, he held murder in his heart. And holds it still. Please, save me from him. He's mad!*

Yes, he thought. I *will* finally save you. Filled with a sudden fierce determination, he rose and leapt at Will.

Will turned, looking alarmed, and drew his hands up to protect himself. The cleaver—*when did he brandish that,* Thom wondered briefly, *and what did he mean to do with it?*—cut into Thom's arm, but not deeply. He felt the pressure, he felt the hot blood, but no pain. He thought James would immediately help him disable the madman, but James had his head turned, peering out into the shadows, saying, "Who's there?"

"Get away from me!" Will shouted, pleading with him.

"You're mad, Will," Thom growled, grappling with Will, struggling to pull the weapon from his grasp.

"She's a parasite, Thom! You said it yourself! She's feeding on you! Why can't you see it?" Will's eyes said: please believe me.

"What?" James asked, bewildered, as he once again faced his companions.

Will struggled with Thom. "Miguel was too far gone to be saved. But I don't think it's too late for you two. Let me help you!"

Thom felt hesitant, filled with uncertainty. His arm was beginning to throb with pain. *Doubting Thomas,* he thought to himself, bitterly. *Story of my life.*

"'Too far gone,'" said James, his voice suspicious. "What do you mean by that?"

"Her roots," Will sobbed. "They were too deep within him."

"You killed him," said James, hatred creeping into his voice.

"I didn't want to! I had to, I was his friend. I couldn't let him suffer."

"Bullshit," said James, viciously. "Miguel was a true friend. He went to jail for me."

Thom blinked. His arm still grasped Will's forearm, but the struggle had paused. "For you?"

James took a deep breath. "I betrayed his friendship. I fucked his fiancée," he said, filled with self-loathing. "Then I killed her." He looked at Thom, but didn't meet his eyes. "You were there. You saw."

"What?" said Will and Thom in shocked unity.

"But you," James said to Will. "You murdered a true friend, you hateful bastard. *I'll kill you!*"

Will tried to pull back, but Thom still held on to him, maddened by confusion. What was true? What was real anymore? He tried to decide what to do: to help James or Will, to run away, to try to defuse the situation so that they might figure out what was really going on.

In that hesitation, Will tried to wrench his arm away from Thom just as James landed a roundhouse punch accompanied by a strangled scream. Thom felt the shock go through Will's body, and the cleaver twisted and cut hard into Thom's chest, the force cracking a rib as Will's body pushed against his own, the cleaver wedged between them.

Thom fell to the ground in shock, his extremities already growing cold. Just like Emily's death, he thought. I'm dying now, I'm actually dying . . . He could see two shapes struggling as his vision clouded red.

He awoke in the cemetery, alone, and felt that warmth of a new day's sun as it lay across his face. He sat up and examined himself, but he could find no evidence of the wounds he was sure he had suffered. He lay just beyond the lengthening shadow of the orchid. Its blossoms were out, and its thick, almost cloying aroma wafted on the gentle breeze.

"Am I dead?" Thom wondered aloud, starting to rise.

"I don't think so."

The response gave him a start, and dread began to squeeze at his throat, for he recognized the voice. "Em?" It was barely a warble, and he felt a fool for even suggesting such an insane thing, but he knew that he was perfectly right even as the single, sordid syllable leaked from his lips.

She stood just over his shoulder, and Thom turned to take her in. She looked radiant, her corn silk hair diffusing the light of the sun even as it accentuated the dark eyes that hinted at mystery, and something more. The face was the exactly the same one that Thom had seen so many times in so many dreams and nightmares over the years, and it was also very near the one that stared back at him from the mirror each and every morning. Her presence, her *immediacy*, captivated him. Electric joy sang its way up his spine.

"I'm sure your wounds are insignificant." She looked away. "I should know."

"Are—are *you* dead?"

She laughed then, a mirthless little sound that chilled Thom's heart and described ice to his veins even as he tried to find reason to laugh along with her. "Do I look dead to you, lover?"

Emily reached down and took hold of his hand, pulling him to his feet. "Give us a kiss."

Before Thom could object, her mouth was implanted firmly over his, and her tongue was winding its way across his own. He had time to appreciate the subtle beauty of the kiss, to admit to himself that he had secretly hoped for just such a moment ever since he was old enough to understand desire, and then he felt the first odd sting upon his tongue.

A picture appeared against the backdrop of his closed eyelids, a remembrance of Emily as a small child. She was sitting out on the back step, licking at a Popsicle that was red, white and blue. The picture stuttered to life, and Thom was instantly positive that he could recall the day; he smiled at the consideration of what came next. He watched as Emily began to tease him with the Popsicle, licking and sucking at the treat in hopes of making him fully appreciate that he hadn't one. As the daydream faded, Thom noted that Emily had proceeded to shove the Popsicle far into her mouth, and that she had begun to choke. Some part of Thom's mind wanted very much to say something about that last snippet of memory, but it was cut short by another sting to the inside of his mouth.

Here was a snippet of Emily, still less than ten, wearing a candy necklace and trying desperately to get some part of it into her mouth. She'd had Thom tie it round her neck for her, and he'd gotten the thing a bit too tight. He remembered that she somehow twisted it in her desperation to suck at the sugary beads, and that she almost choked to death not long after. He didn't need to see a mental replay to remember the particular blue that colored her face when their father had hauled her up from some hiding place she had discovered in the basement.

Thom noticed a crawling sensation inside his mouth even as Emily's tongue probed further. He began to question her motives even as another sting lanced his tongue.

This one brought the recall of an older Emily, a girl who had become a bit more brash, and somehow uncomfortable, even as she seemed to thrive in her schoolwork, and in her newfound extracurricular activities. This Emily wore a cheerleader's uniform, and Thom struggled to place the memory. He watched as she stood in a flower garden, apparently admiring a small rose bush as she caressed a tender petal. Suddenly, she snatched a bee from inside the bloom and rose it to her face. She paused for a moment and studied the insect before popping it into her mouth. She began to chew, and Thom put a name to the wild sensation in his mouth.

His eyes flew open even as he broke the kiss and pushed her away. He doubled over and retched. His efforts produced a thin stream of bile and a single plump yellow jacket, which darted quickly out of his mouth and away across the graveyard.

"Are you trying to *kill* me?" Thom stood and wiped at the spittle that still hung from his chin, his eyes scanning the proximity for wasps. He knew very many things about stinging insects, including the fact that wasps actually called their kindred for help when they were attacking someone. "You know I'm allergic to bees. Christ, I mean, you're allergic to the damn things yourse—"

A dawning realization crept into the back of Thom's mind and began to chat with the other quiet voices there. He looked at Emily, and his face flushed hot with a range of swirling emotions as he turned the newfound truth over and over in his mind. When everything *clicked* and swore its own truth, when he could find absolutely nothing to disprove it, he glared at her for a moment and spoke quietly. "You *bitch.*"

Emily frowned, then cast her eyes at the ground. "I get lonely down there, Thomas. I want my boys back." She leveled her gaze at him. "I want my brother back."

Shocked, Thom just looked at her. He noticed an ant crawling down her dress just below the neckline. "Do you have any idea what you've *done* to us? James is a sullen asshole who shuts himself in his apartment when he's not working. Will . . . Will is just broken—in a bad way, one that might never get fixed. And Miguel—your fiancée—Miguel is *dead*!"

Her head was bowed, but not so much that Thom couldn't see another ant, this one crawling along her cheekbone. As it disappeared from view under her dress, Emily raised her head and looked at him.

"You think I don't know that?" Her voice was low, yet filled with menace. "'Miguel is dead.' Is that supposed to be news to me?" She cocked her hip and rested her arm on it in a defiant posture that Thom remembered well. "I'm bored with him. All he ever does is talk about prison and, frankly, I'm not into homoerotica."

Thom slapped her solidly across the face. His hand came away wet.

She recovered her poise slowly, still on her feet but reeling nonetheless. As Thom watched, though, her complexion began to darken even as her skin somehow dried. Emily closed her eyes and lowered her head, apparently trying to harness the storm that Thom suspected was building inside her. He took a step back, but he wasn't nearly quick enough.

Emily cocked back her head, eyes shut and probably melting in their sockets if her overall state were any indication, and opened her mouth wide to let loose a flurry of insects. Thom began to scream as the creatures alit on him, crawling, biting, *stinging.*

* * *

He awoke to starlight and the shadow of the boneyard orchid, towering and twisting up to the darkened sky. Prone, he could feel the thousand little pricks of dead insects against his back. His sensations told him the insects had come alive, were crawling all over him, but they *couldn't* be. It had to be his imagination, though it lit every nerve end on his skin to think so. The shadows obscured every hint of movement on his body. But there were shadows moving; along with the sounds of a scuffle, the crunch of husks, and a strangled scream.

Will. His voice. "N-no . . . *please*!"

"I'll make things right," a voice responded, hoarse like dry bones grinding against one another.

Oh God, he thought. No. He tried to rise up, but as soon as he did, the pain spread across his chest like razorwire spider webs in his lungs. He clutched his ribs and took a huge, painful breath. His vision washed in reds.

* * *

Emily looked down at him, her face a mask of concern. Thom stared up at her, coughing. "Why?" he got out. "Why have you done this to us? Why did you have to die? Why did you *choose* to die?"

The mask of concern bled away to an expression of soulful sorrow. "It was Will. He found out . . . about me and James. He said he was going to tell Miguel." She turned, looking at the gravestone, warm sunlight streaming through her hair. "I couldn't do it. I couldn't live without Miguel. Or James. You are all so wonderful and special to me. I'd rather lie in the boneyard and be eaten by insects than be separate from my beautiful boys." Her voice remained enchanting to his ear, every word a whispered lullaby.

He wanted to close his eyes and curl up against her, his twin soul, and have everything be all right again.

Thom struggled, slightly, and tried to rise and fight the lethargy. "How could you be so . . . selfish?" he slurred.

"Oh, Thomas, my twin. You were always the strong one, and I was the weaker. I'm sorry, I'm so sorry."

He shut his eyes. No. No. Wake up, he told himself.

Wake up, he heard someone say. A man's voice.

"Thomas," asked Emily. "Do you love me? Do you want to . . . be with me?"

Wake up, the voice said again, almost a growl. His body shook, and Emily faded from sight.

* * *

Thom was looking at dark brown eyes knitted with imposing eyebrows. Black tangled hair framed a wide, puffy face. The man looked stern, but most bearded men did. "Good," the man grunted. "You're awake."

Thom tried to breathe, but each deep breath sent spasms of pain through him. "Will," he gasped.

The man gave a solemn look. "I don't think he made it. That boy of Emily's killed him. But I got him, I did. I got him good." His voice sounded cold, empty of emotion.

Thom felt sick with panic and misery. Will! James! Tears blurred his vision as his heart raced a million miles an hour. He fought to control himself, then tried to rise. "Who . . . " Gasp. "Who are you?"

The large man had turned to look over at the shadows of what must be the two corpses of his friends. He glanced back. "You don't remember me, Thomas?" he rumbled.

Thom shook his head.

"I'm a botanist. I collect rare orchids. I tutored your sister."

* * *

Thom could feel his unsteady heartbeat in the throb of pain that spread like spider webs from his ribcage. He tried to keep his breath deep and slow. The large figure had risen, looking back at that rare flower whose roots dug deep into the earth in front of Emily's grave. *He killed James,* he thought as his heart filled with bilious hatred. He knew logically he had no chance against this guy, not in his condition. The man was larger than him. Probably stronger.

"It's amazing how much you look like her," the man rumbled thoughtfully, gazing between Thom and the plant, as if he could see Emily in the blooming flowers. "Though I guess it shouldn't be. You're twins, after all." He shook his head after Thom didn't respond. "I was always so jealous of you, back then," he confessed. "Emily had a way of making connections with people, individual, intimate connections. I always wanted more. I wanted her heart in my hands." He turned now to face Thom, the crease of pain at the edges of his eyes. "I could never have that, not what I wanted. And I watched you, saw that sullen teenaged boy who had such a connection to her beauty and took it *so much for granted* . . . " He opened his mouth to say more, but stopped himself, reigning his emotions in check. He turned and slowly walked towards the graveyard flower, his back to Thom.

Thom made a methodical effort to quietly rise, wincing in pain now with every breath. When he twisted too far he could feel a line of pain across his side where the cut had been.

"Now I finally meet you," the man rumbled, "and I feel nothing. Nothing save the danger she brings us."

"Danger?" Thom rasped painfully. He limped over. "What do you mean?"

"Your sister, she's a parasite of some kind. And this . . . this flower is some kind of physical manifestation. But I think, I think it's always been there."

Thom glanced from the man's thoughtful face down to the shadowy bodies at the roots. He looked at Will's face, staring up at the sky. It's as if his expression was frozen in time: the mixture of pain, rage, and fear were trapped there, forever.

"How . . . how did this happen?" Thom asked, glancing back at the flower.

"I don't know," the man confessed. "I should, but I don't." He reached out and touched one of the fronds, his reach hesitant, almost worshipful. "She was always fascinated by the strange flowers, the odd facts. The carnivorous flowers, the immortal ones. The legend of the blood orchid, and those New Guinea myths about flowers feeding on the souls of men." He shook his head. "She interrogated me on the insect eating ones, then flew into a rage when I told her there was no evidence of flowers that ate bees. It made no sense to me. Bees and flowers are in a cycle of symbiosis. They rely on each other. They cannot exist without one another." He furrowed his brow. "Their lives, their existence, are as twins. How could you separate that?"

Thom wasn't listening. His mind worked furiously. Immortal, soul-eating flowers. Parasites who consume only part of their host, weakening them but not killing them, allowing their food to live so that they may continue to feast on them. Symbiosis, immortality, denying death, overcoming death. But at what cost?

What have you done, Emily?

He felt a surge of helplessness inside him, spinning and cycling chaotically inside him as if his insides had been replaced by a hive of wasps. He looked slowly up at the bearded man, and said quietly, "How do we stop her?"

The man's shadowy face grew set. "I don't know. If you kill her food sources, she might not be able to survive. If she's somehow connecting to the people she had strong attachments in her life, once they are gone . . . she might not be able to survive. But the problem is, I think we are her food sources."

He turned to face Thom. Thom took a step back, his heel crushing a few more husks. He glanced down at the bodies at Emily's gravestone, their dark blood mixing in with the roots of the great flower in front if it.

"I could do it, I could get you, but . . . " The large man shook his head. "I don't know if I could get myself as well. But then, perhaps I'd end up in jail, or on Death Row. Maybe the state would do me in anyways."

"What if you're wrong, though?"

"I have to take that chance! The dreams, the guilt, everything—it has to stop. *I have to get her out of my head!*" He started moving towards Thom. Even in the dim starlight Thom could tell this man's coherency had taken a redeye flight across country. Thom tensed and inadvertently gasped for air. A mistake as waves of pain lacerated him once again.

Suddenly, the bearded man was illuminated by the glow of a flashlight. Harlan's steady voice rang out, "I think there's just about enough of that," he said, calmly.

Thom turned, squinting into the light. He could hardly see the old graveyard caretaker until he moved closer to Thom, still pointing the flashlight at the large, bearded man. Once the light was no longer directly shining in his face, he noticed that Harlan had something—probably a shotgun or a rifle—cradled in his other arm. He inhaled on a cigarette and gave the bearded man a laconic glare. "Maybe you should just stay calm, while we wait for the police to arrive."

The botanist gave Harlan a thoughtful look, squinting his dark eyes. After a second he seemed to come to some kind of conclusion. He turned to Thom and gave him some kind of knowing look, tapping his nose and mouthing something. Then he turned to Harlan. "I don't think you'll do anything, old man."

"Now, now," said Harlan. "There's no need to get testy here. You're already in a mess of trouble."

"Exactly," the man rumbled, then with a wild look leapt upon the stooped caretaker. Thom watched, stepping forward to do something, anything. It all happened so slowly: the large man rushed Harlan, who raised up the rifle. The blast was deafening, and seemed to shoot out a flash of many sparks. It stopped the momentum of his assailant, who staggered back and then slammed down to the ground along with the sound of a thousand husks crunching sickly.

Thom fell to one knee, gasping. He could hear Emily's angry screams inside his head. He tried to will her away, and failed. He looked up. The old caretaker looked shaken and shocked; as white as porcelain.

The large man moved, suddenly, turning on his side to face Thom. In the flashlight he could see the blood that had stained his mouth, and his wild, dilated eyes. "Do it," he hissed at Thom. "You have to! You can't let her, you know you have to!"

Harlan looked from the fat man back to Thom, his expression widening into a dazed confusion.

Thom gave the botanist a hard stare before slowly sitting down. "No," he said with some effort. "No, I don't."

The fat man looked shocked and angry. Some hidden, fanatic rage swept up through him. He lurched upwards for a second, and desperately staggered towards Thom, bloody hands outstretched. He took two steps towards Thom, then collapsed once again on the ground in front of him.

"I won't," said Thom, fiercely. He could hear Emily, ecstatic, someplace distant, just out of reach. He slumped down himself onto his knees and reached to the ground, picking up the husk of a long-dead insect. He stared down at it through bleary eyes. "I won't," he repeated again, then crushed the insect in his hand.

* * *

It had taken so long to settle things. The investigation stretched onwards until the police felt satisfied with their findings. The two broken ribs he had seemed to take forever to set. The funerals, so many of them, like Emily's funeral all over again. Relatives he hardly knew called to console him. Friends from high school, family members of James, Will, and Miguel, all wanted to talk to him, to reminisce.

The house at first refused to be sold, same with the car. And the packing: so much of his family's stuff remained there, the accumulation of generations. His room, his parents' room, Emily's room, the room of his aunts. Every part of the house had served multiple purposes during his family's stay. And now it was all coming to an end. It didn't seem fair: he had such an attachment to the place. But perhaps that was for the best, that was why he needed to do all this: to close things off, once and for all. To start again, to be reborn.

Emily invaded his dreams, and sometimes his thoughts. There were times where he thought he heard her desperately reaching for him somehow. But it could be his imagination. He didn't trust his thoughts anymore, and he was sick of the constant doubts he had once lived his life with. He would not live in the past, like Will. He would not live in denial, like James, nor allow himself to be beaten, to give up, like Miguel. Nor would he flail desperately in acts of defiance, like the botanist. He would be himself, he would keep moving towards his goals. He would be himself, solely himself, from now on.

He wasn't certain he could do it, but then again, there was a reason James teasingly called him Doubting Thomas.

He had finished packing and throwing things away when the phone rang. He picked it up and answered.

"It's me, Harlan," the voice creaked. "So, you really leavin'?"

"Soon enough. Just a few things I need to take care of."

"Ah, well. Just wanted to let you know, I've been watching that grave you visited after it got cleaned up. Nothing's been, ah, growing there. Figured you would want to know."

"Thanks," Thom said, and he meant it.

"So, what're you going to do now? Where are you going to go?"

"I'm not quite sure, just travel for a while. Not put down any roots anywhere. I've half a mind to go out to the desert, some place far away from humanity."

"Eh, I'm betting I would too, after what you went through. You leaving today?"

"Yep."

"You gonna stop by the graveyard before you go? You know, that grave of hers, it looks much better now with its companion. Kind of . . . makes it seem less lonely there, somehow."

Thom wanted to, desperately. He felt like wires were attached to his chest, pulling his mannequin heart towards Emily's grave once again. "N-no," he rasped out. "Don't think that would be a good idea."

"Well, thought I'd offer. You take care, young man. Write me a post card, from wherever you end up. You have my address."

"I'll do that," Thom said quietly. They said their goodbyes and he hung up.

Thom moved into the kitchen, grabbing one last box. He stepped into the backyard with it, finding the makeshift fire he had set up. Ten minutes of work and some scrupulous additions of lighter fluid, and he had a large fire burning. He pulled out pictures from the box, Emily's diaries, her old personal effects, their yearbooks, and started throwing them on, one by one.

He emptied the box and stared at the fire for a bit, frowning. He felt brokenhearted, worse than any breakup or failed relationship he had ever had. He tried to tell himself, *this is good for you. The pain says you're healing.* But he wasn't sure he believed it.

He pulled his wallet out of his pocket and opened it up, removing a picture he carried there. It was from high school, a picture of the gang: Will off to one side, smiling hesitantly as he looked at the others. He looked tall and thin, with a prominent Adam's apple he lost later in life. Thom was laughing at a joke—the actual joke lost in memory. He stared at his feet, looking as if his shyness had momentarily cracked but was hastily being repaired. James was between Thom and Emily, arms possessively around both of them, head down but eyes looking up with a sly, almost whimsical smile on his face. Emily stared right at the camera, her gaze and expression were as if she was in the here and now, but trapped in the picture somehow. Miguel filled out the picture, one arm around Emily's waist, his mouth open as if talking. The picture caught him in mid-blink, with his face upwards towards the sky, as if he was breathing in the air and shocked by how pure and wonderful it was.

It took forever for Thom to throw the dog-eared picture into the fire, but he did, and the picture lit up with a spark of greenish flame before withering and turning black.

Thom stood for a while, then doused the fire and turned back inside, locking the back door and calling for the cab. He moved his bag out with him to the front porch, and waited for the car to show.

It didn't take long. The cabbie was a boisterous man for whom English was only tenuously a second language. Far too often it seemed to drift into complete unintelligibility. Thom didn't mind. He closed his eyes and leaned back in the seat. The car drove away from his family house, and Thom didn't look back.

GONE IS THE WIND

Gary W. Conner

First there was the click, which was far louder than he'd ever imagined it might be. It carried so much weight, it bore so much resonance, that he almost backed out.

He gathered his resolve, found his determination, and then there was another odd sound. It was deafening and, in the fleeting seconds between recognition and oblivion, he considered the end, and all that preceded it.

* * *

Padgett came awake to the undulating chipping and churring rhythm of the battered ceiling fan above his head. It was a comfortable noise, and Padgett rolled over in the bed, one arm searching out Ellie. Her side of the bed was empty. As he came to full awareness, he remembered why.

He reminded himself that he was twenty-eight, that he'd once owned a black cat named Vanilla. He recited the prayers he'd memorized years before, and he wept another time for those he'd lost along the way. Mostly he wept for Miriam, a daughter lost much too soon, and his wife, Ellie, taken much too slowly.

There were times when he wanted to scream, but the room

seemed airless, and he was unable to offer wind to his denial.

When he finally found the emptiness, he rose and made himself ready.

* * *

A few years before, his neighbor, a nice woman named Isabel, had introduced herself at an old-fashioned ice cream social organized by a neighborhood group. There had been a new twinge of feeling in an otherwise numb Padgett, and he'd engaged in conversation with her for hours. They ended the evening by dancing for the first time; while Padgett could not remember the name of the song, the melody would never leave him. He had fallen in love, again, somehow.

They were having coffee one morning at a nearby fast food restaurant when Isabel mentioned that she was doing some work for a program that delivered meals to elderly shut-ins. "The 'Senior Assistance Plan,' they call it. I suggested 'Eats on Feet,' but they cringed at the connotations."

Padgett frowned. "I tend to agree." He smiled then, glossing over the disruption in their normally agreeable circumstance as he sugared a fresh cup of coffee. "So, then, how does your program work?"

Over the course of the next hour, they sipped at hot coffee as Isabel unknowingly showed Padgett a path to her heart. Before they called for the check, he'd agreed to help out with the delivery of meals, and he delighted Isabel with his suggestion for a new name.

"Perhaps you might call the program 'Meals on Heels?'"

Her face had come alight, and a smile widened her delicate features. "That's brilliant! Would you mind if I suggested it to the managers?" As she reached to caress his hand in a reactionary touch, as he fell in love for the second time in his life, he could only smile and offer tacit permission.

Padgett remembered that it had been especially windy that night, that the air seemed ready for murder and mayhem. He recalled mostly that he nearly ran home in his glee, that he was winded yet quite well when he found himself on his doorstep. He smiled at the memories, then let himself out of the flat and wandered down the avenue. He would go to the Center and he would pick up the day's meals, and he would hope against hope that he might see Isabel just one more time.

* * *

Padgett followed his usual path, a carefully planned route that led him first away from the Center and then back to it. As he rounded past a shoppe on the first leg of the journey, he was surprised to see someone lying on the sidewalk. The figure was swathed in a throwaway rug colored with faded and stained earthtones, with only a spill of hair at one end to suggest gender.

Padgett instinctively slowed, but too late. A hand shot from beneath the covering and grabbed him by the ankle. He struggled to free himself as the blanket fell away to reveal a man rising to a sitting position. Padgett exclaimed his surprise in a shrill, short bark of a scream and struggled to free himself from the man's grasp.

"Hey, guess what?" The man struggled to rise, then staggered toward Padgett as he found his feet. His face was covered in grime; the rivulets of sweat weaving their way down it served only to enhance the shine borne of poor personal hygiene. "I put the wind in the trees."

The man leered at Padgett, then suddenly turned and resumed his place among the many.

Padgett gave traffic a mere consideration before he darted across the lane. The darkening sky began to make good on its promise of rain as he was midway through the short escape, and he pitched his morning paper over his head in an effort to ward off the fat drops. At the curb, he paused to turn around and glance back at his newfound nemesis.

The man seemed to catch his gaze, for he suddenly sat erect and screamed at Padgett. "I put the wind in the trees! I put the wind in the trees!"

Padgett found a corner and turned it, the rain falling against his face and mixing with the strange sweat that seeped from the pores in his scalp and ran in curving rivulets across his face. His strides were long and dangerous, given the grime of the sidewalk and the growing downpour. Yet, he made a few hundred before he paused to consider the food parcel, slowly growing all the more damp tucked only beneath the meek protection offered by his outstretched arm. As best he could tell, nothing had spilled or even tried to: the slight bag offered no particular scent or stain, and the weight still seemed appropriate. Unmindful of the diminishing rain, he used his free hand to pat all the pockets that had claim to his possessions. Satisfied, he tossed the sodden copy of the *Times* into a bin and continued down the route.

A glance at the only slightly damp checklist—stored carefully in a pocket during the short squall—revealed that Padgett's next stop was with Mrs. Kelley, a kindly old woman with no specific malady beyond a general case of advanced age. Padgett thought that perhaps the old girl clocked in at something like a hundred-and-four, but he could never nail it down.

He climbed the short entryway and rapped lightly upon the door. It swung open only after interminable minutes, and it did so very slowly. The heavy wood with all its intricate and convoluted power swung away to reveal a frail, tiny woman. Her skull was evident, and hid only beneath a thin layer of tired flesh. Her lips parted in a smile that very much wanted to be a grimace. "Oh, Freddie, how nice to see you. Please come in." She stepped aside and gave Padgett a clear path to the ancient dining table located off to one side of her cramped living space.

"Ma'am," Padgett nodded as he entered. The woman's tiny flat was evidence enough for the cost of living too long, and Padgett tried hard not to notice the squalor as he crossed to the table to lay down the meal. He set the bag upon the peeling formica, wondered briefly if the cheap alloy legs would support the weight. It held, and he reached into the sack. "So, Mrs. Kelley, I've heard that you've taken on a runabout."

She shuffled across the dirty linoleum—the neighborhood seemed to be papered in it, and Padgett could not recall the last bit of carpet he'd seen, but for the bedroom in Mr. Keagan's flat. That bit of rug had been threadbare and shrinking from the walls, to be sure, but it was carpet nonetheless.

"What's that you've got there, dear?"

He piled aside two other cartons—the stack wasn't sorted to his route, and he grumbled again after haphazard fashions—and found the one he was after. "It'll be a nice cut of fish with some celery and a bit of soup." He set her carton aside and began to repack the bag. "So, that runabout? You've taken one in?"

The old woman beamed proudly, and Padgett found himself glad of it.

"I have," she said.

"Where is this one, then?" Padgett patted his pants pocket, reminded himself that he carried more than one type of dinner.

Mrs. Kelly turned and called out.

Padgett could not help but smile. "You named this one 'Purpose'? Bit of an odd name for a cat, to be sure."

She looked at him, a gleam in her eye that reminded him that she was not dulled, despite her advance in years. "Not all that odd. He shows me things."

Just then, a skinny tabby entered the room. Its steps were tentative, small, and the animal was clearly distrustful of both Padgett and its newfound host.

"Ah, this will be him, then." Padgett stooped and drew a tin of cat food from his pocket. He eyed the feline even as he drew back the peel-away lid of the can and set it on the floor, as far from himself as his arm would allow. Purpose came slowly across the room, sniffing at the air now and then, perhaps fixing direction, perhaps looking after distrust. At last, it found the tin and began to eat voraciously, even as it exchanged glances with Mrs. Kelley and Padgett.

Padgett rose and turned to Mrs. Kelley, offering a smile. "We've got to stop taking in these strangers."

She stepped next to him and laid a hand on his shoulder as she continued to look at the cat. "You know I can't help it." Her hand slipped down his arm until it was entwined with his own, and she raised their arms in emphasis. "That cat, Freddie, that cat is something else. The things it tells me—sometimes it keeps me up at night... but I feel like I should know everything *it* knows, right?"

Padgett took a step back toward the table, back toward his packages, yet he maintained eye contact with Mrs. Kelley. "I'm certain that we can always learn." He offered a glib smile, then broke contact with her and scooped the bag off the table. "I need to get on, Mrs. Kelley. Be sure and heat the fish properly, and the soup as well. Don't want anything to get rotted."

She planted a hand on either side of his head and drew his face down for a wet kiss on the cheek. "Thank you again, Freddie. You're such a sweetheart. Someone like you, still only a widower—I'll never understand it."

She walked him to the door, then called after him as he made his way down the short, cracked and crumbling cement that was her walk. He turned and retraced a few steps in the direction of the small doorstep she stood on. Absentmindedly, he realized that this was the first time he'd ever seen Mrs. Kelley outside of her house. He'd never realized, not really, that she was far too skinny for her frame; that her hair was an almost striking waxy blue color; that her housedress was at least ten years old. "Ma'am?"

"Freddie, you stay clear of people you don't know. Someone is out for you. Purpose told me, and I don't much like what he said."

Padgett offered her a smile, hoped that she'd make good use of the food on her table. "I'll be careful. Do the same?"

She nodded slightly, and he set off on his way. A check of the list provided him with Mr. Grove's address and meal number. His brow wrinkled; Grove was a nice enough fellow, but his flat reeked of vomit. Padgett had never seen the man vomit, and he couldn't imagine what the source of the awful smell must be, but it never failed to squirm his stomach.

He set off down the avenue and rounded the corner onto Twelfth. As he strolled down the wider sidewalk, the smoother surface offered by a street that did more important things than pass through this little neighborhood, he thought back on the days he spent rolling dice in back alleys to pick up just a little something extra for the week ahead. He'd lost more than he won plenty of times, but the only thing he could clearly recall now were the wins, no matter how small or shamed.

He came to a curb and waited for the pedestrian signal. Ahead, the sign for Corner Billiards still hung from its routine post above a storefront that had been abandoned for thirteen years. The light turned, and Padgett jogged across the lane—even though he didn't want to overexert himself (the day was still young, and there were still many miles to cover), behind-the-wheel mercenaries abounded. His heart pounded a little harder as he stooped to catch his breath on the other side of the interchange.

He finally captured his wind and stood straight to free up his pinched lungs. He immediately noticed that the old billiards hall had suffered a whitewash. For countless years, Padgett had come round this corner and been able to spy directly into the hall. He'd watched his friends shooting a game or two through those windows; once, he caught a glimpse of a reviled foe glaring at the table while Padgett's old girlfriend stood by, waiting to hear what she might do next to please her new boyfriend. He'd even watched a man get shot in the gut and bleed to death on the sweet felt of a favorite table.

Even after old Mr. Freeman closed up shop and retired to a fifth a day in front of the telly, the view into the place was marred only by the yellow grime of a million spent cigarettes. Now, however, someone had seen fit to paint over the glass front. Even the door had not escaped attention. Padgett wondered over this for a moment, until a disturbance in the lower left corner of the coating caught his eye. He took a few steps forward and stooped for a better look. Someone had scraped away parts of the paint to form two short words:

HELP ME

He peered at it, puzzled. Suddenly, more of the paint began to flake away and disappear, and Padgett could make out the long, thin, strangely blue nail that picked the letters out. He was too stunned to move as he watched the letters being carved: First an "F," then an "R," and then an "E." When the first "D" appeared, he stood and raced to the door. It was surprisingly unlocked, and he threw it aside and ran into the interior of the old storefront.

Something was very wrong, *askew*, and Padgett stopped to get his bearings. In a brief moment, he found the discord. The place was stacked with furniture, wall-to-wall and sometimes floor-to-ceiling.

"I apologize for the disarray." The masculine voice came from over Padgett's right shoulder, and he whirled to get a look at the owner. He found a man in a suit that might have cost good money, yet might be a knock-off.

Padgett gaped at him for a moment, then closed his eyes and took a deep breath. "I'm sorry," he said, opening his eyes once again. "I didn't realize anyone had moved in."

The man seemed vaguely familiar to Padgett, even with the oiled hair, the slick suit, the fancy watch—the odd tattoo on his wrist. Padgett gave it as much attention as he could before it slid back into the man's cuff.

He shook his head again, tried to gain some sense of bearing on this new conversation. "I just stepped in from the street." He offered an apologetic smile. "I—I thought I saw someone scratching at the whitewash."

The man sprouted a frown. "Pardon me?"

Padgett turned and swept out an arm. "The whitewa—. . ." He stuttered the sentence to a stop as he looked through the clean and clear plate glass to the other side of the street. A woman pushed a tram around a particularly nasty spot of sidewalk. A man stood near the corner reading the day's news. A car rolled slowly by, obviously adherent of the stoplight that protected the intersection. Padgett spun back around to face the apparent proprietor. "Wh—when did you move in?" He twisted his hands together. "Recently?"

The man took a step toward Padgett, then put a hand on his shoulder. He leaned in to whisper, "I still remember you."

Padgett felt his face flush, and he drew away. "Whatever do

you mean?"

The man offered a sardonic grin, then he turned and swept an arm toward his goods. "Anything in the place—yours for the asking." He stepped aside to pull a wicker chair from a stack of furniture. He eyed Padgett eagerly. "Do you like this? It's certainly handsome. Perhaps it would work well with some of your other furnishings?"

Padgett suddenly found the weight of the bag dangling from his hand, remembered the urgency. "Thanks, no, I have to go." He took a moment to appraise the man before him, to commit him to some small corner of memory, and then he turned and left the building, turning right and looking for his bearings. A garish pink stucco huddled in the shadow of the tenement, and it was accompanied by an even smaller unit, this one disused and falling into mere memory.

A dog began barking somewhere across the street, and Padgett found his pace quickened without any clear intent. Somewhere in the distance, the air was disturbed by a sharp crack, and Padgett briefly considered a poorly adjusted carburetor before his mind fell away to other things.

* * *

He sucked in air as quick as he might, but it seemed to do no good, to serve no concrete purpose. He occasionally thought that he should probably exhale at some point, but every time the notion surfaced he found that he had little or nothing of which to rid himself. He seemed to be capable only of sucking in the world around him, offering nothing in return. He soon identified an odd hiss and his hand found the source as it clamped onto his chest, trying desperately and almost subconsciously to seal the gash.

Black spots formed before his eyes, and he began to grow dizzy.

* * *

Padgett pounded again upon Mr. Groves' door and he

wondered, not for the first time, if the old gent had finally given way to time. He could already sense the aroma of disarray leaking from the crack below the doorstep, and he wished again that he might have the old man removed from his route. He rubbed at his nostrils in an unconscious attempt to separate himself even as the door finally fell aside to present the object of his visit.

Mr. Groves stepped out onto the portico, and Padgett did his best not to stagger backward in distaste. He swallowed carefully, afraid of what might come rumbling out of his inners in the face of such unbearable stench.

Groves smiled with a handful of teeth, most of the remainders yellowed with smoke and bad food and age. "Come to see me again?"

Padgett did his best to return the smile, then he thrust forward a shortened bag for the taking. "Yessir. A nice meal, here." He drew a breath from over his shoulder. "Some mashed ham, some potatoes, even some gravy. I'd think you might enjoy it. It's certainly good for you."

Groves continued to offer his diseased and crooked grin even as he accepted the bag. "You're a fine lad, Padgett. It's a shame what happened."

Padgett nodded, unsure, but careful to shorten the encounter wherever possible.

Groves seemed to have different designs, however, as he leaned suddenly into Padgett and offered a conspiratorial whisper. "We'll miss you. Take care with what comes next."

Padgett stood on the doorstep for just a minute more, unsure of what to make of Mr. Groves' behavior, wondering if perhaps he should report the aging man to some sort of nursing authority.

Groves raised a hand and extended his finger, reaching toward Padgett's head.

"Can—" He looked to Padgett, seemingly seeking some sort of approval. His hand hovered alongside Padgett's right ear. "Can I touch it?"

Padgett drew back in a cringe. "You've your meal, and I've other people to see. It's best we both get about it."

The old man fell glum, and eyed the package swinging from his hand. "You're right, of course. Best to you." The door swung shut against Padgett, and he was glad of the barrier. He turned and ambled down the short walk, trying to make sense of what had just transpired.

He bounced the bag in his hand, trying to guess the number of stops left by the simple weight of the package. He passed the short gate and ran headlong into someone standing on the common walk. He looked up to offer an apology and saw a face he could place no further than today—yet it was a face that had plagued him throughout this short day. "Who are you?"

The man stepped back and raised a hand in supplication. "No harm, friend."

Padgett noted the tattoo winding around the man's left wrist before it disappeared inside the man's sleeve.

Padgett abruptly met this new encounter with an anger that surprised even him. "What the fuck are you doing?" He advanced upon the man even as he noted that the hair was no longer oiled, that the brow was somehow softer, that the man's ear was no longer pierced.

Padgett's newfound adversary, apparently convinced that he was dealing with some sort of lunatic, quickly turned and jogged down the lane, turning the first available corner. All the while, Padgett screamed after him but did not give chase.

As Padgett tried desperately to find his wind, he noticed a scrap of paper lying on the tarmac, ostensibly left in the stranger's wake. He took a moment to collect himself, to bring his heart rate under control, and then he stooped to retrieve the snippet.

On his haunches, Padgett carefully straightened the bent edges of the paper then read the enigmatic inscription aloud: "Regent's Park. Eight taken." He knew the grounds well, but he could draw no sense from the rest. He stood and thought again about giving chase.

Deciding against it, certain that it would now be a waste of time, he instead pocketed the tiny testament and pondered over approaching the police. They might surely think him mad, he reasoned, but the fact remained that he was in some form being harassed by someone who seemed capable of altering his physical identity on short notice—but not so much that he became unrecognizable to Padgett, his apparent quarry.

He decided to locate the nearest pub and take tea, to mull over the day's weirdness and hope for a solution to what seemed to be an incomprehensible malefaction. Old Mrs. Yorke was next on his shortening list, and he knew a place not far from her flat where he might gather himself. Thus decided, he drew a deep breath and set about his course, determined to find his wind, to get on with his bit.

* * *

The small tavern occupied an older building, and it described itself in unflattering terms. The name was The Flagging Tendency, and the stout was described as "mediocre but drinkable" on a signboard out front. Padgett's request for tea was met with guffaws from not only the keeper but several patrons as well, and he finally settled on a pint, though a secret worry over his charitable position still gnawed at his gut. He took a seat in a tiny booth near the back, as far from the windows—the street—as the place allowed. He found little solace in the distance, and yet he took a deep draught from the mug before attempting to catch his unruly breath and thus settle his nerves.

He worried the door time and again, searching for the face that had belabored him throughout the morning, even as he checked and rechecked his list of visitations to make certain that he could keep his schedule. Yorke was a given, as she was all but around the corner; Tippen likewise, as his place nearly intersected Mrs. Yorke's; Reikhard was something of a stretch, but Padgett felt he could manage it. That left only Frasier, a youngish woman touched with a fear of the world. While Padgett certainly sympathized with her circumstance, especially given his own present situation, he feared that he'd have to cross her off the day's list.

Time nagged at him as he sipped again and again at his first pint and then even a second, and he grew increasingly worried about Mrs. Frasier. She seemed most likely to go without a meal, and thus she was the one who might need his delivery the most. At times, he was angry with the oily-haired man for robbing him of his ability to perform his charity; at other times, he was mad at himself for allowing it. At the end of it, he was decided that he would deliver Mrs. Frasier, skipping the others in favor of getting home to his flat and nursing the illness that must surely be overtaking him.

After his third pint, he left a few pounds on the table and wandered to the doorway. He blamed the alcohol for his odd stagger, for his sense of bewilderment.

* * *

Mrs. Frasier passed her waning years in a flat adjoining Regent's Park, and this fact was not lost on Padgett as he banged on her door loudly enough for her to take notice and heed his call. He looked again and again over his shoulder, sure that his pursuer would suddenly appear at the edge of the grounds, some sort of malice in hand and ready. As it was, the door fell aside before any such thing occurred.

"Ah, then, it's just you. Come to bring me supper, have you?" She was a narrow lady, short of stature, yet a woman who wore some sort of thin royalty like a badge. On many occasions, she had explained to Padgett just those royal ties .He had always listened with patience and charm—he prided himself on his capacity for tolerance—but he'd never quite got the gist of it.

Now, she stepped aside to allow him entry, and he made his way past into her darkened quarters, pausing just past the threshold to let her catch up to him and lead the way to the meager kitchen, though by now he knew precisely where it was. He heard the clunk of the door shutting behind him and felt her skeletal arm brush against his elbow as she brushed past, but he was surprised when she turned into the parlor, avoiding the kitchen altogether.

"I've a visitor, Freddie. Please say 'hello.'"

Padgett followed her into the small chamber and was somehow unfazed when he observed his new companion. He felt that he should have screamed, he should have run, perhaps he should have even run screaming, but instead he took the man's proffered hand and shook it, all the while noting once again the oily hair, the tattoo on the wrist, the man's sly smile. "Haven't we met?" It came out in a squeaky whisper; Padgett briefly considered that he'd not really even said it aloud.

The man grimaced. "Of course." He withdrew his hand, and seemed to consider Padgett for just a moment. "I'm afraid the outlook isn't good."

Padgett was understandably taken aback, and he glanced quickly at Mrs. Frasier, then returned his gaze to his condemnor. "I—I'm sorry. Whatever do you mean?"

"Surely you know that you're bleeding badly." The man's eyes again scanned Padgett's body before settling upon a direct stare. "I wish I could be more optimistic. Have you found God?"

Bewildered, Padgett looked down upon himself, curious as to what might cause this stranger to offer such a dire pronouncement, and he was shocked by the sudden profusion of blood that poured from ugly wounds that he was unaware of, astounded by pain that he did not feel, gashes that he could not explain. He crumpled into the arms of the oily-haired stranger.

* * *

First there was the click. It was produced by the brass buckle on his clarinet's case, and it seemed to echo out over the grounds at Regent's Park. The sound, the sheer magnitude of it, lent weight to the initial fear he'd experienced when confronted with the idea of joining the Royal Greenjackets Band. He'd never played for anyone but himself—and his wife, and the occasional close family member—and the thought of displaying his musical worth in front of thousands of complete strangers was not one he entertained with any sense of fondness. It was, however, a secret dream, and one that his wife knew well. Eventually, due mostly to her constant urging, he'd overcome his fear of public persecution and he'd signed on with the band. Now, however, his wife's keen words were long forgotten, and he knew only the scrutiny of the public eye, the discordant opinion of the people.

He thought again about how he might somehow back out, how he might close up his case and run nearly screaming from this gathering in Regent's Park, but he gritted his teeth and promised himself that he would weather it.

He gathered his resolve, found his determination, and suddenly the wind was sucked from him even as he felt an odd sort of nauseating compression. During a strange and protracted moment of eerie agony, he felt the weight of each and every organ he carried—and then his vision went black and his brain smashed against the side of his skull. In the fleeting seconds between recognition and oblivion, he considered the end, and all that might come after.

* * *

An insistent pressure on his neck and a quiet voice brought him awake, dispelling the vivid memories of wife and daughter that had been carousing in his head. He opened his sluggish eyes to stare into the face of the stranger who hovered over him. He took note of the man's hair, slicked back in a sort of ducktail that defied his years, and of the thin tattoo that encircled his wrist. He picked up his head to get a better look and saw that it was really only a medical bracelet, perhaps some sort of identification.

"Freddie?" The stranger's voice was mellifluous, yet tinged with panic. "I need your attention here."

He laughed, and a spray of blood erupted from his lips for the effort. "Frederick. No one calls me 'Freddie.'" A red bubble formed on his lips and popped into a spray as he coughed. "Though I don't suppose that I mind it all that much."

A wrenching pain pronounced itself from his gut and demanded attention, so he screamed against it.

The stranger appeared in his line of vision once again, this time mere inches from his face. "I need your attention here, no matter what you call yourself. There's been an explosion—it seems that someone planted a bomb under the bandstand. You've been hurt very badly. I'm afraid that you may be dying. Your lung is punctured, and you've lost a lot of blood. How are you feeling?"

Padgett opened his mouth to speak, but was rewarded only with a fresh gurgle of blood. Once it was spilt, he found his voice. Through increasingly agonizing pain that he was only just beginning to realize, he said, "I'm not well, if that's what you're after. I'm dizzy, and I can't seem to get my wind." He coughed up a bit more blood, less this time. "Be good to see the family again. Nothing here for me, really." Every attempt at breath only hurt him more, and at last he found that he could no longer try.

He lay alive on the grass surrounding the bandstand for a few minutes more, and then he quietly passed in the afternoon hours.

In quiet, tiny corners of London, commoners with surnames like Frasier and Groves and Yorke found themselves brought to tears, even as they struggled to find a reason.

BEYOND THE BLACK

Gary W. Conner & Brett Alexander Savory

Black.

Seeping through.

Creeping under blankets. Filtering in through pores. Crashing through bone. Ebbing between synapses, brainwaves, cranial fluid. Devouring, usurping.

There is only the absence of light.

Black.

And my son.

Jamie!

Clawing his way through dirt. A digging corpse. Bloody nails, eyes, teeth. Dead . . . but dreaming . . .

Dreaming and digging—

—out of his own grave—

into a blinding swatch of moonlight . . .

Black. *Just that one word.*

I'm coming, son.

Then, something beyond the black. Just a glimpse. Not even fleeting, but nonetheless burned into his mind, engraved into the matrix—an afterimage, dissipating, melting, then slithering away, bathing him in cold sweat and waking him, his son's name slicing his vocal cords, slicing the cold night air whispering in through the open window near the bed, slicing his heart into tatters as he remembers lowering the coffin into the ground two weeks ago.

The drive to the cemetery is through an eclipsing chasm of grief so deep, even the night seems to lose its way.

* * *

"Bury me, you coward!"

"I can't, Jamie. You know I can't."

Moonlight trickled like syrup through the trees in the graveyard, and lit the boy's sharp features, face turned up, screaming at his father.

"Bury me, or I'll kill them both, Henry. I'll kill. Them. Both. Do you understand?"

Henry Pickstein shuddered and looked away. He thought of Joanne, his wife, and his daughter, Molly, felt tears threatening. He turned his attention back to his only son.

"Why are you doing this, Jamie?"

Ten-year-old Jamie Pickstein's eyes, lit by something malign, didn't blink, didn't waver, as he answered: "You know why, dad." A sneer lifted one corner of the boy's ashen lips. "I have to find the way back. Beyond the black."

Henry blinked and tears rolled down both cheeks at the words. "No, son . . . you don't have to go back there. You can stay with us for a little while. Don't you want to come home?"

Laughter, like the rustling of dead leaves, fell from the boy's mouth, cut off abruptly by a fit of coughing, followed by a thin trickle of blood that ran over his bottom lip and dribbled down his muddy chin.

"Why would I want to come back?" Jamie said quietly.

"Because we're your family, Jamie," his father said automatically, the words hollow.

More blood trickled down Jamie's chin. He turned his head and spit a gob of the stuff onto a discarded spade jutting out of a cold mound of earth, his gaze lingering, getting lost in the 6 x 6 hole in the ground beside him. His glassy eyes stared *through* the ground, into the realm he had been ripped from such a short time ago. He could still smell the scents of that place, see the burnt, decaying landscape, feel the oppressive atmosphere weighing him down.

Down into blessed peace.

No thoughts came to him in that place; nothing but the texture of the ground beneath his feet, the wind across his cheek, and the steady, ominous thrumming that reverberated through his body from some unknowable source.

Somehow, Jamie Pickstein had come back from the dead—

(for a purpose, jamie—don't forget your purpose)

—and now he wanted to go back.

"I have no need for a family, Henry," Jamie said, deadpan, the use of his first name instead of "dad" making Jamie's father cringe inwardly.

What had happened to his little boy?

Jamie glanced at the open grave again, then back up to his father. "You have no idea what it's like, so you can't understand, Henry." Jamie's eyes were nearly glowing now, backlit with crimson and hate. "So either put me back in that hole and bury me again, or walk back to the house with me and watch me murder your wife and child."

(be careful with the child, jamie . . . remember . . .)

Henry was shaking uncontrollably, head spinning, his rapidly blinking eyes darting about in his head, searching for useless words, words he knew could change nothing. Something had stolen his little boy, and all that was left was his empty body and his voice.

"So what's it gonna be, Henry?"

Henry was still foundering for words, more tears flowing down his cheeks. What was he to say? *Okay, son, I'll bury you alive, no trouble. Anything for my best boy!*

Jesus.

Then something occurred to Jamie, and his eyes darkened with the thought.

He gazed up through the skeletal trees, and rested his arm on the spade sticking out from the dirt. "You know, I could just as easily kill you and force *mom*"—he said the word like it was rotted meat—"to bury me. I'm sure she'd be easier to convince. 'Specially if I cut up her daughter. What do you think, Henry? Think she'd do it if I did that?" Jamie chucked a dark, rattling noise out of his throat and winked at Henry, licking blood from his bottom lip. He lifted the spade up slowly from the mound of dirt, keeping his murderous gaze glued to Henry, whose eyes were widening with every inch the spade came free.

"Jamie, no . . ." he breathed, staring back into those soulless orbs and knowing that this thing—whatever his boy had become—would kill him without a second thought . . . and then slaughter the rest of his family, if they, too, refused to help him.

"Jamie, why don't—" Henry gulped, trying to buy time, trying to think of anything that would convince his son to just come home with him and forget about all this killing, forget whatever place he had seen in death and wanted so desperately to get back to. "Why . . . why not just do it yourself, if you have to? Why do you need us to help you?"

"Well now, Henry," Jamie said, slipping the spade free of the dirt, and taking it in both hands, hefting its weight. "That's about the stupidest thing I think I've ever fucking heard."

(*besides, it's not time yet*)

"Bury myself? Now, tell me how to go about that, *dad*. Go ahead, you stupid bastard. Tell me." Jamie stepped forward from the edge of the hole. He swung the spade over his shoulder and continued walking toward Henry, who shuffled backward, nearly tripping over branches and tombstones.

"Don't you think I would do it myself, if I could?"

(*not yet, jamie*)

Jamie continued, the intermittent moonlight now dappling his pallid skin as he moved deftly over jutting stones and thick, creeping tree roots. "I need one of you."

Henry stumbled and cursed, never taking his eyes from the spade resting on his boy's shoulder; those last five words fumbling around in Henry's mind, tripping over their own jutting stones and creeping roots.

Overwhelmed with grief and battered by images of the past ten years, Henry stopped where he stood, swaying, waiting.

Jamie lifted the spade high, and the dead whispered forgotten prayers in a thousand different languages.

(*I need one of you . . .*)

The spade fell, bone exploded inward, blood arced into the moonlight. Then a hundred souls ripped Henry's spirit free of his body before the next blow could connect. His body fell to the ground and leaked its life into the sodden dirt.

Jamie Pickstein dropped the bloody spade, walked through the cemetery gates, and headed home.

* * *

Two days later, Molly Pickstein was cleaning her room—again. At seven years old, she had found a certain sense of satisfaction in a neat room. It pleased her mom and dad, and that pleased Molly. She was just about finished, her bed tightly made and all of her dolls and teddy bears carefully placed just where they belonged.

Not a thing without a place, and not a place without a thing.

"Shut up," Molly said, dismissing Jamie's voice in her head. She found that Jamie often had a lot to say about any number of things, but no one except Molly could hear him. Jamie had always talked a lot before he went away, and now seemed to be no different. Mom would call him a "noise box," like she always used to, if only she could hear him.

The room cleaned to Molly's standards, she crossed it and opened her jewelry box. Flipping the shiny brown lid up, she adored the treasures of her short lifetime. Two faux-pearl earrings that she had borrowed from her mother's own jewelry box years before; a golden stud that Marcus Owenfield had given her two years ago after he'd found it on the street in front of Madison Grocery; finally, and most importantly, the necklace that Jamie had given her—the one that sometimes glowed at night, a figure-eight Möbius loop—a symbol for infinity—dangling from its centre.

The necklace scared Molly because it showed her things. Mostly good things, like eating an ice-cream on the Fourth of July, or riding her bicycle down Ryan Street, the wind batting at her face and making her hair fly out behind her head—but sometimes there were bad things. She put the chain around her neck, positioning the loop just so.

With the loop in its place, the noise she'd been hearing since they'd lost Jamie flooded her senses. That awful noise, like the churning of gears, an awful screeching noise—*gears that need oil.*

Gears turning. Unstoppable.

Molly slipped between the covers of her immaculate bed, turned off her bedside light, and fell into a fitful sleep, her breathing keeping time with the sound of the gears.

* * *

When Molly awoke, she was thinking of her father's car.

She dressed quietly and made her way down the winding Georgian staircase that connected the two halves of her life. Her mother was nestled in the tiny kitchen that served as the trough for the Pickstein family. She was peeling oranges, throwing the rinds haphazardly into a wastebasket positioned near the sink.

Molly sat quietly at the table awaiting breakfast. A sudden thought struck her. "Mom, where's Daddy?"

Mother dropped the knife suddenly to her side and turned. "You know that he's gone for a few days. He has to eye the orchards and what not. You'll see him soon, I promise."

Molly frowned, unhappy with her mother's answer. Mom made a lot of promises that didn't always come true—as of late, they were true less and less of the time. Molly figured that she wouldn't see her dad tonight, or any night soon.

Always worried about dad. Why don't you ever worry about me?

"Shut up, Jamie."

Mom spoke from the sink. "What's that, dear?"

"Nothing, Mom."

* * *

After a long summer day filled with chores—and a little idle time thrown in here and there for good measure—Molly found her mom in the kitchen preparing dinner.

"Molly, dear, dinner's almost ready. Would you set the table, please? I've got to go check on the laundry."

Molly did as she was told, being careful to place the forks on the left side of the plates, and the spoons and the knives on the right.

When her mom came back into the kitchen, she observed the settings. "Molly, why did you set three places? You know your father won't be home for dinner tonight."

"It's not for dad. It's for Jamie. He's coming home tonight—he told me to set him a place."

"Molly, sit down please." Mother took a seat at the table. Once Molly was seated, Mother said, "Honey, Jamie is never coming back. We've had this discussion. Jamie is with God in Heaven."

"But, mom, he talks to me sometimes, and he said that he's coming to see us tonight, and that he's bringing us a surprise."

Tears seeped from the corners of Mom's eyes, and she said, "Molly, maybe you better go to your room for a bit. I'll call you when dinner is on the table."

"All right."

Molly slipped from her chair, looking downcast, and walked slowly up the staircase to her bedroom.

Mother lowered her head to the table, resting it on her crossed arms, and wept—a long, slow, quiet hitching of breath. She didn't want Molly to hear and become upset.

Upstairs in her room, lying on her back on her bed, Molly tried to forget about her mother's terse words and focus on Jamie's surprise. What could it be? Molly couldn't wait to find out. Soon, she was so excited she was physically shaking, wriggling about on her bed, a big smile spread across her face.

She wouldn't have to wait long, though, she knew. With her necklace's aid, in her mind's eye she saw Jamie walking down the road. It was a road she recognized near their house. Maple?

Maybe Birch? One of the surrounding tree streets, anyway, for sure.

She closed her eyes and thought of her father's car again. It was parked somewhere . . . there were a lot of trees around. Close by on one of the tree streets? No, it was too shrouded, no light coming through. There were little blocks in the ground close by, she could see that. What are those?

Tombstones, silly, someone whispered. Jamie again.

Her eyes flashed open and she sat straight up in bed. She looked quickly around her room, but there was nothing, only the whispering of the chill wind through her open window. She got up to close it . . .

. . . and saw Jamie coming down the street toward the house.

He's here! she thought. *Finally here!*

She whipped around and took off like a shot out of her room. She descended the staircase in twos and threes.

Barreling through the kitchen doorway, she yelled, "He's here, Mom! He's here!"

Mother lifted her head slowly from her arms, tears glistening, bangs matted to her forehead, dinner forgotten and burning in the oven. "Wha?" she muttered, too consumed with emotion to understand the significance of the words.

Molly yanked on her mother's arms, straining like mad to get her out of her chair. "He's *here,* I said!"

Molly was angled backward, feet slipping on the linoleum floor, her face red with effort, frustration. "Come . . . *on!*" she said, yanking harder. "He'll be here any—"

The doorbell rang, cutting into Molly's pleading whine.

Mother frowned. Molly finally stopped pulling, smiling ear to ear. *Jamie's back!*

Then a different image sliced into Molly's mind's eye. Not daddy's car, nor Jamie's playful face and words. Something she had never seen before. A wasteland of sand and scorched earth. Something humming far off in the distance, or maybe right in her ear. *Where is this?* she thought, fear slithering through her mind. *This is nowhere* I've *ever been.*

Mother pried Molly's fingers from her forearms, turned toward the front of the house, tried to see who it was through one of the side window slats that ran up the length of the door. She peeked around left, then right, her frown deepening. She hadn't noticed that her daughter was mentally somewhere else.

In this wasted place, Molly turned around to look behind her to see if there was anything else she might recognize. But there was only more of the same . . . except that there was something far away, too far away to see clearly. Spinning. It was . . . falling into itself and reappearing, the sound of the thrumming that underlay everything, emerging and dissipating with the sight.

A knot formed in the pit of Molly's stomach and she doubled over in the middle of the kitchen in pain. With every reappearance, the thing seemed to get closer, and the pain increased. "Mom . . . ?" Molly whispered hoarsely, unable to produce anything louder from her constricted vocal cords.

Something was very wrong here. She didn't know what, exactly, but she could *feel* Jamie in this other place, knew instinctively that he'd somehow been there. As Mother got closer to the door, the loop on Molly's necklace glowed like the sun.

Mother reached the door, closed her eyes, grasped the knob. She twisted it slowly, then pulled when she felt the latch release. When the door's arc widened enough to see who it was, she opened her eyes. The color drained from her face.

"J—Jamie? Baby?"

"Mom, please let me in. I'm cold."

Mother sputtered a little more before Jamie pushed the door open wider with one hand, and with the other grabbed a fistful of hair at the back of her head and slammed her face against the hard wood of the door. She collapsed to the floor in a heap.

Molly backed up slowly until her outstretched hand found the railing at the foot of the stairs, just out of sight of Jamie and the bleeding shape on the ground that was her mother.

"Molly? Moll, is that you?"

Molly stared wide-eyed, her breathing shallow as she crab-walked her way up one stair, then two.

"Molly? Ya gotta do something for me, sweetie."

Molly whimpered, crawled backwards up three more steps. She remained silent and stayed where she was on the staircase.

"Remember that necklace I won for you at the fair? Wasn't that nice of me?" She could hear Jamie's footsteps in the kitchen getting closer to the staircase.

"Well, Molly, now I need you to do something nice for me. I need you to put me back where I came from."

As quietly as she could, Molly stood, turned, and made her way up the rest of the stairs. Once at the top, she carefully approached the railing and leaned over. Below, she could partly see Jamie, standing on the first step of the staircase.

Drawing a deep breath, Molly called out. "Jamie, why are you here?"

There was a nasty grin pasted to her dead brother's face. "Why, Molly, dear, so good to finally see you."

"Wh—what do you want?"

"Well, now, it seems I need your help. You see, that idiot father of ours decided to dig me up. For what fucking reason, I don't know. He had no idea what he was doing interrupting my journey like that. I have things to tend to back in my new home. Very important things."

Jamie started slowly up the stairs, listening to the voice from beyond the black whispering its desire in his head, testing each step as though it might be the advancement that would send Molly running. "Moll, I need you to do one simple thing for me: bury me. Do you think you can do that? I need to get back, sugar. Do you understand?"

As he got closer, Molly could see the small insects crawling around his eyes. The maggot that had escaped his leering mouth and was now traveling toward his nostril. The flies that buzzed around his head. The way his hair was matted against his forehead and slicked with the seepage of rot.

"I *have* to get back, baby girl. Things will go all to shit otherwise." He stopped four steps short of Molly, who stood open-mouthed, dazed by her brother's state of disrepair.

Then, a slight noise.

Gears.

She raised her hand to her necklace and touched the loop. As she stole a glimpse at it, it suddenly flared with a bright orange light, and her thoughts were stolen away into a world of nightmares worse than the one she faced on the staircase of her home.

The place of sand and heat

(*welcome home, molly*)

the place of sun and pain, the place where hell came rolling along like a groundhog with a slinky for a skeleton. The place that consumed, the place that never forgave. As she scanned the horizon, she saw a dune collapse upon itself, only to reemerge out of the ground, only to collapse upon itself once again.

It was coming toward her.

"Are you going to help me, Molly?" Jamie now stood only two steps down from her. The skin of his face was pasty, doughy—his cheeks sagged, making him look like a sick bulldog. One eye seemed destined to fall out onto Jamie's cheekbone, seeking to follow its fellow facial muscles in a parade down his face. She noted that one of his ears was partially eaten away, that the soft yellowish-white of cartilage had begun to show itself in a number of places.

"Molly! Are you going to help me—or do I have to kill you, too?" She heard Jamie's voice as if from behind a wall.

Mom's dead? Molly thought. *But he only hit her once . . . She can't be dead. She can't be—*

Again: *gears.* Louder now.

They seemed to hesitate for a moment, almost to bind, but they quickly came loose and began spinning madly. The noise was now almost unbearable, and all thoughts of her mother spun away with the gears.

The tidal wave of sand, the climbing/falling/churning thing was almost upon her, and she looked quickly about for shelter. Finding none, she turned to face the sand.

When it rose only feet from her, it again collapsed in upon itself . . . and did not reappear, only a slight breeze marking its passage.

The noise was gone. She turned around slowly, looking for the machine, but it had vanished.

She snapped back to reality, the Möbius loop on her necklace no longer glowing, and saw Jamie standing scant inches from her on the staircase.

"You have to put me back, Moll," Jamie pleaded, now drained of his aggression, only a scared little boy, just doing what he was told. With the shield down, Molly could see it in her brother's deep brown eyes. She saw what now lived in Jamie's body.

Not a thing without a place, and not a place without a thing.

"It's me that it wants, Jamie," Molly said, clutching the loop. "Not you. Me."

Then she was back in the world of sand and heat again. The gears ground together, starting up beneath the sand. It was right under her. And it was inside her, a part of her now, too.

(*welcome home, molly*)

Something dripping and hot rose from the sand between her legs, and she moved back a pace to get out of its way. Something twisting and mulching like a drill. Sand spun off it in all directions, and she knew she should be frightened, but fear was not going to come this time for Molly. There was only the sound of the machine and whatever was dripping from the bit as it spun around and around.

Jamie just watched his little sister at the top of the staircase, deflated, no longer needed, unwelcome. He could not see what was happening to her, but he knew where she was. It was where *he* wanted to be, where he *deserved* to be.

He moved to touch her, to shake her out of it, to get back what was rightfully his. When his fingers touched her skin, the drill quickly angled sideways in the sand and drove into Molly's rib cage. She felt its heat raging through her and, upon Jamie's contact, his eyes bubbled and boiled in his skull. Pustules formed and popped on his desiccated skin, and then his head exploded in a shower of red and white. His corpse tipped backward and fell down the stairs, the hand that had touched Molly blackened, scorched.

The drill entered her deeper, probed into her heart, and spoke:

(*not a thing without a place, and not a place without a thing*)

Molly, covered in gore, crumpled to the landing of the stairs and her heart stopped beating.

She did not hear the police sirens. She did not hear the ambulance. All she heard was the distant thrumming of an engine, and the turning of well-oiled gears.

* * *

When Molly next opened her eyes it was to complete darkness. She hitched in a sudden breath, but then relaxed as she heard dirt falling on her coffin from above.

Home, she thought.

Then she closed her eyes, felt sand and machinery pulse through her blood, heat burn the chamber of her heart, the Möbius loop singe her pallid skin where it lay around her neck.

She whispered her brother's name.

And thought she heard him whisper hers.

ANNIVERSARY OF AN UNINTERESTING EVENT

Brett Alexander Savory

A young man sits in the chair across from me. We're seated at the dining room table. The young man has a black pen and a yellow pad of lined paper in front of him. He leans over, picks up the pen, and writes.

* * *

Today's the day. And no one's here but me.

I know they didn't just forget, but it's tempting to delude myself.

How long has it been? Five, six years? I suppose I should keep better track.

Doesn't matter, though, because I always remember the day. And that's more than the rest of them can say. I can't recall the last time everyone gathered together for this anniversary.

I'm the only one who cares.

My brother, the Great Explorer, is probably gallivanting around the world, uncovering pirate's gold or scaling treacherous mountains. What a gem he is. What a wonderful guy to consistently miss this anniversary. You'd think it'd be important to him. You'd think it'd be important to all of them.

My sister, well, she's probably at home with her fuckhead husband and three screaming troglodytes. Three thousand miles away. They drink wine out of crumpled Coke cans, and watch *Happy Days* reruns every Saturday night. Their dog only has two legs—the front ones—and the troglodytes laugh as it drags its ass around the living room. Their mom and dad ignore them, and concentrate on The Fonz working his magic on the jukebox.

Where the wine-out-of-a-Coke-can habit came from, I've no idea. But then, how their dog wound up with only two legs, I've also no idea. No one tells me anything.

My mom? Well, mom's old and getting older. She thinks Jewish people are taking over the airwaves, tells me to stop watching the news because it's nothing but 'Jew propaganda.' Good old ma. Her eyesight isn't so good, either—keeps bumping into walls, falling down stairs. It's a wonder she's even still alive. But her hearing's okay, so she could at least call, for fuck's sake. Even though no one lives here anymore, I keep the phone hooked up.

Just in case.

And finally, dad: where's he? Why isn't he sitting at this table with me? He should be here for this. Should be here to hold my hand. Tell me he remembers, that he's sorry, that everything's going to be okay. But he's not here.

He's not.

* * *

The young man sighs, puts the pen down beside the paper, leans back. His eyes glisten. The air is empty around him—he doesn't feel what he hoped he would, doesn't feel much of anything at all these days.

The young man tears off the sheet of yellow paper, places it gently in the middle of the small, round table, pushes his chair back, gets up and leaves the dining room.

One year passes.

The young man enters the dining room again. Pulls out the chair across from me, sits down. The pen and paper are still right where he left them. No one has been here to move them, because no one lives here anymore.

He closes his eyes slowly. When he reopens them, the pen is already moving across the yellow pad.

* * *

My father wasn't a very nice man at all. I suppose I can't really blame everyone else for never showing up. I think the last time everyone was together here at this table was—god, it must be nine, ten years ago. So why the hell am I here? Why do I keep coming back?

I ask myself that question every time I jump in my shitty little car to drive up here, this forgotten house, this decayed little room. Why? What's the point in coming back when no one else does? It's not like he was nice to me when he was shitting on the rest of the family. We all got shit on equally. So far as I can remember, he was never nice to anyone—not friends, family, neighbours, or strangers.

But I'm here again, aren't I? And I don't even know what I'm hoping for, writing these stupid, pointless notes. He can't read them; the only one who reads them is me. I've written five or six of them now, and placed them all in the middle of this table. Words on top of words—letters to a dead man.

I remember three or four years ago my globetrotting brother called me to ask if I was going to the old man's place again that year. He called from fucking Peru. What a dick.

Anyway, I said yeah, I'm going to dad's, then what I said next I said before I can catch myself—already feeling my face redden before the sentence is completely out of my mouth: "You should come, too, Paul."

He laughed. Hard. Like it was the most ludicrous idea he'd ever heard. Like whatever the hell was there for him in Peru was more important than remembering his father. But family never has meant much to Paul. Only airplanes hold meaning for him. Only hotel rooms. Exotic food. Exotic whores. Anything North American is shit; he'll have nothing to do with it. And that includes his family. We're not from Venezuela; we're not from Spain; we're not from Asia. We're from Marthaville, Ontario, Canada. Not a person of ethnic origin for farm field after sprawling farm field.

So he laughed at my suggestion, and I wished he'd been within arms reach so I could strangle him. And I fucking would—I'd wrap my hands around his throat and squeeze until he was dead.

He laughed until he was out of breath, then just as he was about to say something, I hung up.

We haven't spoken since.

I told mom about the fight. She pretended she couldn't hear me. I told my sister. She laughed and said, "Well, that's Paul, you know." As if she were any different.

Then I told dad.

I told my dead father about the fight. I spoke aloud to this empty room, described the argument word-for-word, then waited for him to take someone's side. Of course, there was only silence—just like when he was alive. He never chose sides between us. The only side he ever took between his three kids was my sister's, if Paul and I were doing something to bug her. But if the trouble was between Paul and I, dad suddenly lost his voice. He wouldn't take a side, no matter what. He'd just tell us to work it out ourselves. And if there's one thing I hate him for more than any other, it's his inability to choose between his sons.

I can forgive everything else. But never that.

I don't think Paul ever cared, though. If he did, he'd be here now. Writing reams and reams of repressed bullshit on lined yellow paper. Trying to raise the dead.

* * *

The young man tears off another sheet of paper, places it in the center of the table with the others.

Sometimes he makes coffee, but most of the time, it's tea. He puts a little bit of milk in the tea, never too much. This is the way his father used to drink it.

Occasionally, the young man looks up from the piece of paper he's writing on, looks right at me. But his eyes just pass through. He complains that no one's here to share this anniversary with him, but I'm here.

I'm sitting right here.

But I guess it's not enough. He wants more than this. And I

can't blame him, not even a little. Fathers are very important. Especially to their sons. Daughters can grow up, get married, find another man on which to lean, to depend, to fall in love with. But sons only have their fathers, and sometimes their brothers. But usually, there is only one shot to make that kind of connection.

The young man gets up from the table, goes over to the kitchen, and makes another pot of tea.

When he pours himself a cup, he does not put in any milk.

While he sips from his cup, I rummage through the small pile of yellow paper in the centre of the table, pull one of the earlier sheets from the bottom of the stack. He does not notice.

I lean back and read.

* * *

Third year in a row I've come here. Again, there's no one else. Maybe they think what happened was my fault, and they can't bear to be around me. Too harsh a reminder. Or maybe I look too much like him. Probably doesn't bother Paul or my sister, Jill, but my mother—she's pretty far gone, and I'm not sure what she sees when she looks at me now. I just know that whenever I look in the mirror, I see dad. I don't see dad's eyes, or eyebrows, or nose, or mouth, or any particular feature—I just see dad as a whole. Maybe that's why I want to father my brother, straighten him out, force him to settle down.

He flew to Scandinavia this year. Sent me an email from the hotel he's staying at. It read, "Sorry I can't come with you to dad's house, bro. Lots of business to take care of over here. Hopefully Jill makes the trip out; you really shouldn't be going there on your own. It's not healthy, you know? Anyway, say hi to mum and sis, if they show. Let them know I miss them, and I'll try to visit soon."

I wrote him back a long, hate-filled letter, filled with condemnations about his irresponsible lifestyle, his apathy toward the rest of his family. I ripped into him so hard that by the time I was finished, I was crying, hitching in violent sobs, my chest aching like hell. My finger hovered over the Send button, shaking, tears dripping onto my keyboard. But then I highlighted the letter, hit the Delete key, indented once, and wrote simply

"Fuck you."

And hit Send.

He did not respond.

I miss Dad so much. Why can't I be the favourite? Why can't he pick me? I'd say I'm waiting here for some kind of sign, but that's not true. Dad never was one to give hints or indications about his intentions, thoughts, feelings. But I also can't believe that he was just some soulless rock carved in the form of a man. Carved in the form of my father.

He must have loved one of us more than the other; love is discriminating and never doled out evenly.

If I could send an email to Dad, I'd tell him to fuck off, too.

* * *

I lean forward, put the yellow paper back where I found it. Not that I have to bother, mind, but I like to at least *feel* as though everything is back in its proper place.

The young man is about halfway through his tea, and stares over my right shoulder as he drinks. He looks at nothing on the wall behind me. Fading orange wallpaper looks back at him.

Breaking out of his usual pattern of writing a one-page letter, then drinking tea and leaving until next year, he sets his cup down gently on the table.

Something inside me moves ever so slightly and the telephone rings. He does not answer it. Instead, he very deliberately rips another page from the yellow pad of paper, brings it toward him, and positions his pen to write a second page.

The phone stops ringing when his pen touches the first line.

* * *

This will be my last visit to dad's old place. Dad is not here. Dad is not coming back. I never really thought he was, of course, but still, it bears saying aloud: He's not coming back because he's dead, and that means his legs can no longer support his weight. But though weightless, he somehow still sits on my chest. Strangely, it is not an altogether uncomfortable feeling.

But I'm sick of buying tea at the little convenience store around the corner. I'm sick of sitting in this chair, waiting for silence to smother me. I'm sick of wishing someone would come here with me, keep me company, mourn the day. This is Dad's special day more than his birthday ever was. This day signifies everything he was to me, to Paul, to Jill, and even to my mother. It's the day he showed us he was never going to change, never going to apologize for anything he did. There was a sort of sick form of hope rotting inside each of us, holding on, wondering if the day would ever come when he'd take it all back. Ask for forgiveness.

I'm sick of thinking thoughts like this. The weight is too much.

I want to go out like Dad did.

Careful where you tread, son; don't go sayin' things you'll regret later. Sure won't, Dad. I always listened to you when you said dumb shit like that. But I just want to die now. I want to die like you did. Right here in this fucking kitchen. I want you to be *made* to choose between your sons, because I know you won't do it on your own. Because you're a coward. Always were. So why don't I choose for you? You can't give me a good reason not to, because you're a completely unreasonable man. But I loved you when no one else did.

And now I'm whining . . . fucking pathetic.

The wine in Coke cans was from you, wasn't it? You started that with Jill, shared it with her and only her, excluding Paul and me. And your travel bug was shown only to Paul. Books about it, National Geographic specials, Discovery Channel. Right? I'm right, aren't I? Fucking prick. What do I get? Huh? What do I fucking get??

The muzzle of a gun in the mouth. That's what I get. And maybe that's what I want. A fucking—

The telephone rings again, startling the young man. He glances at it quickly where it hangs on the wall, pen hovering over the page, vibrating. His eyes are wet with tears. Face red, sweating.

He stares at the phone, frozen. It rings and rings.

What you already know is that the young man staring at the phone is my son; what you don't know is that I did love him. I loved him very much. More than my wife. More than my other son, Paul. More than my daughter, Jill. But I was wearing someone else's skin. It fit poorly, and every crossroad in life to which it brought me showed me two choices—neither of which was good for my family. Neither of which was good for me. So I chose from this other man's list of options. This skin thief. And it was always wrong, no matter what I did, no matter how I felt or what I did to try to create alternate options.

You see it on your anniversary. You see the darkened shadow of your skin. The son you created; the son you forgot. The son you never meant to hurt.

But.

I'm tired of being the scapegoat. I'm tired of having everything blamed on me—the way he turned out, the way my family turned out. All of it. Tired of hearing that it's all my fault, and no one else did anything wrong. Just heartless, soulless Dad, fucking everything up, making life miserable for everyone. It's a load of shit, and seared into my brain I have a list of transgressions that my family made against me—every button pushed, every boundary crossed that made me blind with rage.

It's a leap of idiot faith to think that when you forget about the dead, the dead forget about you.

The phone keeps ringing; the pen stops vibrating.

It has been so many years, son. Pick up the phone.

The young man sets his pen down. He pushes away from the table, stands up, walks over to the phone. He brings his hand up to the receiver, lifts it gently from its cradle, puts it to his ear.

I hope he hears my voice.

There's something I desperately need to tell him.

WALKING

Seth Lindberg & Brett Alexander Savory

Walking. The sun beating my back like a fist.

Sand swirls around my feet. Pick one foot up, set it down. Swirl. Pick the other up, set it down. Swirl.

I don't trudge through the sand, I walk. This sand is old and deserves at least that much respect.

I have walked for fifteen years. I don't remember a time before my feet moved this way, taking me places I want to go, places I don't want to go.

I feel alone when the sun goes down. When it's beating on me, I feel alive. I feel like it's driving me on. If it's driving me toward something in particular, I don't know what it is.

And I don't want to know.

I lost my tribe four years ago. Or my tribe lost me four years ago. I woke up one morning and everyone was gone. Two cantinas of water were left beside me in the sand, with a note that read, "The time has come."

I left the note behind, and I left the water, too.

I pass through small villages sometimes. People see me, my parched, sun-blackened skin. My cracked and bleeding feet. They offer me water, thrust it in my face. I say "thank you" and push it away.

I don't need their water; I stop at mirage oases and drink as much as my belly will hold.

These people try to touch me after I refuse their water. They brush their brown fingers along my black skin. Cringe. Mutter to themselves. Back away slowly, eyes wide. No one walks after me once they've touched me. They just let me go, happy I'm not staying.

I've never stayed in one place for more than a day. The disadvantage of this is that I've gone through my entire life knowing no one but my tribe; the advantage of this is that I've gone through my entire life knowing no one but my tribe. I do not want to know anyone. I didn't even want to know my tribe. But they were my brothers and sisters. Some by blood, others by experience.

The night they left me, the wind hadn't been blowing very hard, so when I woke up and found them gone, I followed their tracks as far as I could. They went in a straight line, over hills, into valleys, fading with every step, until I lost them. Covered by sand. Swept away by wind and the desire to be free of me.

I had done nothing to them.

Nothing.

So when their tracks ended, I sat down behind the last footprint I saw, and watched until the wind and sand erased it. Once it was completely gone, I scooped my left hand into the place where the footprint had been, lifted the sand to my mouth, and swallowed it.

I rose to my feet, feeling the burn from the sun on my back, pushing me forward.

I walked.

And have not stopped walking since.

* * *

Tiny black specks on the horizon. Another town, growing as I approach it. Its people lined up to greet me.

I wonder what they have heard about me from others. Am I someone to be feared? Am I the walking dead? What stories have grown around me? I would ask these questions as I pass, but I am unsure what will come out of my mouth should I open it to speak.

The tiny black specks become shapes wavering as the heat rises from the cracked ground. There is shade there, and the people are dressed in white robes embroidered in a tempest of bright colors, colors I can only just make out. I see the men of the town, some shading their eyes, some smoking, others cradling old, worn rifles. The women sit in the shade. Many of them have rifles, too. Children, playing together, kicking a ball around. A dog barking in the distance, somewhere in the town.

Forever goes by slowly, with the plodding of one foot after another.

I have a slight limp these days, from two years before I passed over the mountains. The route up was exhausting, but the pass down the other side proved more treacherous. One false step and I tumbled; I do not know how long. But the pain in my left leg moved like lightning up through my body when I put pressure on it. I cried, I screamed myself hoarse, I called out to God, the sun, anything that would hear me.

I stayed there, lying on one side, until the sun went down. My left leg swelled and grew purple. At night, the dreams that always haunt me took on renewed strength. I awoke and saw a shadow on the rock. A man, looking off in the direction I was going. Eyes shaded by a wide-brimmed hat. No moonlight touched his face. In his lap rested an old sword, glinting slightly.

"It's not time yet," he told me, looking out across the desert.

"Who are you?" I asked.

"It's not time yet. Keep walking." He rose, and without making a noise, turned and leapt off the rock and into deeper shadows. I fell back to feverish sleep.

* * *

I am close enough to see their faces. Hard and worn and weary. Eyes like crystals set into craggy rock. They look lean and angry, but their expressions are bored. Those that have rifles don't bother to raise them at me. They don't know what I am, what I bring.

Word has not spread as fast as I thought.

I pass through the small crowd at the edge of town, blackened skin smoking in the sun. One woman opens her mouth to speak; the man beside her turns his head, looks at her hard. She closes her mouth, the question still in her eyes: *Why have you come?*

I cast my eyes down; I have no answer for her.

A small boy breaks the grip of his father's weathered hands, scurries to meet me. I stop, look down. The child looks up, says, "What happened to you? Why do you look like that? Where are you going?"

I look to the boy's father, smile at his son's innocence. The man does not smile back. I bend down to speak to the boy. "My skin has been damaged by the sun," I say. "And my tribe abandoned me a long, long time ago, so now I just walk. It seems the right thing to do."

The boy frowns, reaches out tentatively to touch the crisped skin of my shoulder. His father moves a step closer, calls him away from me. The boy does not listen. His brown fingers brush lightly against my flesh. His lip curls up, and he pulls his hand away quickly. His eyes lock to mine before he dashes away, back into the protective hands of his father. Where before there was one set of hard eyes coming from the direction of the boy and his father, now there are two. I wonder if the boy is scared because of my appearance, or because of something he might have felt when his skin touched mine.

I feel that both time and the sun have burned me; one blackens the skin, the other blackens the soul.

I stagger forward, the weight of the boy's eyes slowing me down. A man's cold stare I can handle, but the children always weaken me.

Other people come out of their huts, out from under crumbling wooden porches. Some point, others sneer. Some just stare, with that burning question on their lips. Even if I had an answer for them—a true answer—about where I'm going, I wouldn't tell them. Not a single one.

It is no one's business but my own. Mine, and the shadow that follows me.

From the last porch on the edge of this little town, a few young women offer water from the safety of their huts. I look up, but see in their eyes not concern for me, but concern for themselves. They are selfish, offering me help only to appease their consciences.

But soon their canteens will fall from their hands. Their bodies will crumple, fall hard to the ground. Their eyes will see nothing; their hearts will see even less. And there will be no one to take them away from here. No one to save them.

The shadow will cover them, hide them from God's eyes. And when the shadow finally passes, lifts from the town, drifts up and into the night, it will be too late.

God will no longer be looking.

Cold, cold eyes that deserve nothing more push me out of town. I do not look behind me, but I feel the whisper of a chill climb my spine, cover my bald skull. I picture the look on the boy's face, the boy that touched me and turned to stone. His father's hand as it falls away from his tiny shoulders. His eyes roll back in his head. Knees buckle, hit the dirt. He leans to one side, already dead. Mouth open, thinking no thoughts. A tiny puff of dust as his upper body meets the ground.

In the middle of the day, darkness falls, covering everything. Destroying in silence.

A shroud from the eyes of God.

I stare up at the blinded sun, the corona a wreath of flames around a blackened disk. It does not damage my eyes. Not anymore. My teeth grind, and I force my head down, staring at the pathway ahead of me.

I see the shadows turn into crescents, the light return slowly. I want to look back at the settlement behind me, but I resist the desire. Force my eyes ahead.

They are now only history's dust.

* * *

Later, the sun smears the horizon with reds of all shades, purples, yellows, oranges—all which fade to gray. Gray that soon fades into the muted colors of night.

I light a fire to simulate the sun's warmth. The sticks and branches I have gathered make something passable, but the fire is weak and hungry, complaining and dancing. Nearly fading. I throw a branch, stir up the coals. It dances into life again, holding on by the barest of threads. It takes such effort to maintain it. But I feed the fire so that I may have company as I drift to sleep.

When I wake again, freezing, the fire's been reduced to glowing embers. And there's another glint, like starlight. I look up over the dying fire to see the man in the wide-brimmed hat sitting in the darkness, prodding the fire with a stick. The old blade lies across his knees, edge out to me.

"You wake," he says.

I rise up on one elbow, suspiciously, try to banish the stiffness from my neck and shoulder, and fail.

"Your sun is dead," he says, his voice dry as paper. He pokes the fading embers with a stick, they light up at once, then dim down again.

There is nothing to say to that.

"In ancient times," he continues, "mankind personified the sun and death by assigning gods to them. In some places, the Sun God was simply a position to be filled. In others, he was the austere ruler. Others still, he was the lord of the midday sun, bringer of pestilence and death, starvation and drought. The Sun and Death were one."

I blink at his blasphemy, and quickly mutter, "There is no god but God."

His chin inclines just a fraction. He sighs. "So people say."

Dogs bark in the distance, and he turns to peer off in that direction. "The cold of the night denies the death the Sun so gladly gives. And the night chases the mad Sun across the sky, never quite catching up. But what will happen when the night does, eh?"

I rise up and watch him warily. He's awaiting a response, but I have none to give. "Perhaps we shall see, you and I." His voice is quiet, like the night air. He stands and sheathes his blade, and makes his way to his horse. I haven't seen a horse in . . . ages. Such a luxury. Its coat is white, almost cream colored, and its eyes are pitch. The expression it gives its master is one of both fear and familiarity. He slides up in the saddle, grasps the reins, and rides off.

The Sun and Death are one, I think.

One I follow; the other follows me.

* * *

When I wake the next morning, I am more tired than I have ever been. My bones ache, seem to grind against each other when I move. It is barely dawn, and the embers from last night's fire still crackle in the small pit I dug in the sand. Although I stand and stretch my muscles, feel more mentally awake, the more I move, the more I stiffen up. Perhaps my insides are charring to match my outsides.

I dampen the remains of the fire as best I can before moving on.

The world tips forward and the sun reels high in the sky as my thoughts spin around each other inside my skull. Thoughts that I've never had before. Alien intrusions to my previous way of thinking. Maybe it's just because of my body's early morning aches, but these new thoughts are sending signals not only to my brain, but throughout my entire body:

Stop.

Stop walking.

But the learned muscles in my calves, thighs, feet, stomach, and back cannot comprehend this notion. It is impossible to stop. It has always been impossible to stop.

I push these thoughts away as best I can, and continue walking.

A new horizon, a new town. The sun is (death)—

I push this thought away, shake my head, blink my tired eyes.

It is not death. The sun is life. It has given me life all these years.

In my mind, a wide-brimmed hat nods slowly. Bared teeth

glimmer beneath it.

I push, and I push. *Get out of my head, stranger. You do not know me. You cannot change what I am, what I do.*

My muscles repeat their patterns. I put one foot in front of the other. The town seems to sprout out of the drifting sand.

I suddenly feel very strongly that I am being watched. I stop abruptly, turn around, scan the endless brown haze.

Nothing.

When I turn back around, continue walking, the voice in my head is so clear, it's as though the stranger is whispering directly into my ear, from just over my shoulder: *The sun represents different things to different people. You are old in its eyes. You are losing your way. You have, perhaps, already lost it.*

I bow my head, but keep walking, determined not to listen. But my bones hear the voice. They seize up even more, as if the sand has somehow gotten inside me, is rubbing between my joints, eroding my ability to push forward.

But I know what walks with me. And I know how to play this game.

At the edge of town, the people have gathered. As they always do. Somewhere nearby, the smell of burnt food wafts on the still, dry air. Today, the townsfolk seem less substantial. I picture storm clouds in their minds, darkening their eyes.

The small crowd parts as I walk slowly through them. I want to speak to them, but I have nothing to say. To me, they are just ghosts, already haunting my future. I envision them as the bits of sand between my bones, slowing me down, commanding me to stop. Live the rest of my days in this little town. Become one of them. Have children—small boys, frail little girls. Raise families of sedentary ghosts, always looking to the horizon for strangers passing through their towns, for the sun, and for what follows both of these things.

More sand shuffles between my bones, changing my gait, turning me into someone else. *My walk is who I am. It defines me, drives me, gives me strength. This cannot change.*

But these unsettling thoughts keep coming, and the thoughts

give life to the sand, which gives life to the stranger, to his wide-brimmed hat, his inexplicable sword. Why would you need a sword like that? Out here? Out here where nothing ever happens. People making people making people making no sense to each other, confused, but driven to walk, move about in some way, some fashion that seems to make sense until the end of the day when they go to sleep, stop moving, and they realize whether they move or not—whether they walk or not—they're going nowhere, because nothing exists out here. Tribes, connections, familiarities, friends, enemies, all of it just sand in the end, just something to be swallowed by the sun, swallowed by death, swallowed by strangers passing through your town, your mind, your heart, swallowed and driven under, dug into the sand, until—

—there's only a little boy standing in front of you, staring up into your face.

I try to push past the boy, but he nimbly evades my hands, steps back in front of me, blocking my way. The townsfolk huddle together around us, looking on.

"Out of my way, boy," I say, not my usual self, the pain in my bones and these strange, intrusive thoughts changing my reactions. I know that he is just a curious boy, but he a curious boy who is in my way.

"Please," I say, trying to navigate around him again, "let me pass."

He just blocks me again, but keeping clear of my reach. I look around again. The townspeople are more tuned into this than if they were just looking on to see what happens. They're staring so intently, I feel the heat of their collective gaze like an animal breathing at the back of my neck. Their eyes pierce the swirling dust, insisting. But insisting what, I don't know.

"Whose child is this?" I ask the people. "Come. Please take him away. I must . . . I must walk."

No one moves. The dust swirls faster around us. It seems to crackle against my burnt skin.

The boy continues to stare up at me. He is maybe nine years old, dark hair, dark eyes. He does not smile, does not frown, but there is something in his eyes and the way that he stands, almost defiant, that reminds me of the way I was at that age. He is a boy that wishes to belong. To something, anything that will embrace him.

A boy that no one wants.

"Take him," comes the first tentative voice from somewhere near the back of the semi-circle of people.

"Yes," says another, "take him with you, wherever it is that you're going. Take him from us."

A few more pleadings, these from women, some stepping forward to lock eyes with me, convince me it's the right thing to do. "He does not belong here," they say. "We do not know where he belongs, but it is not with us."

Others speak of reasons he must go, but mostly there is only the common thread of 'take him, make him go away.'

Sand piles up between my joints. My mind swirls with the sand that blows through my hair, stings my eyes. I feel disgust rise in my chest, followed quickly by anger and decisiveness. I lunge ahead with most of my remaining strength and agility, manage to just grab one of the boy's skinny little arms before he dodges out of the way. I reel him in quickly, then push him hard to the ground.

The townsfolk become silent. I stand over the boy, glaring hard. "Let me pass," I say, and force my muscles to respond.

One foot in front of the other.

I walk around him while he stares up at me, still expressionless.

I'm several agonizing steps past his body when I hear him attempting to gain his feet. I turn around. He gains his feet slowly, brushing himself off, turns to look at me.

I turn back around, and walk.

I hear him follow.

I do not turn around, but say, "Go back, boy. Whatever it is like here, it is infinitely worse out there."

His steps do not slow, do not falter.

I feel the comfortable black shadow rear up behind me in the sky, fall on the town like a dropped blanket.

"Go back," I say. "Go. Back."

I trudge forward, feeling my bones turn brittle, sandblasted, as though they'll snap inside my body with my next step. The boy follows closer.

The shadow envelops the town, making it less than silent.

* * *

The boy pulls up alongside me, a question in his eyes.

"Dead," I say. "They're all dead."

He does not ask how or by whom. He just nods, keeps walking. And again, the stranger's voice in my head: *Stop. It is over. Just stop.*

But I no longer know how to stop. I will grind my joints and bones into each other until they crack and crumble. Or until there is nowhere left to walk.

We walk in silence for a few minutes—he turning his head around every once in a while, checking for any sign of life from the town, me facing forward, knowing the boy will see nothing.

The sun, high in the sky, somehow seems to squeeze its rays under my torched skin, burn me inside, bake my innards, melt my bones. I have never felt the heat of the sun so strong. My breathing becomes heavy. I squint my eyes against the bright sand ahead of us. The boy beside me, soft, light brown skin, appears to feel nothing, soaking up the damaging rays like they're fueling him onward.

I think of my tribe, the day they left—when I woke up, found them gone, having abandoned me. I think of the way things were before that day. The sun now wrenches memories from me, things I had forgotten: the isolation, the loneliness, the feeling that no matter how hard I tried, no matter what I did, I would never fit in with these people—blood relations or not. I was not like them, in mind or spirit. I was something else, driven to *be* something else, by necessities beyond my control. Beyond the control of any living creature.

My pace slows, the sand in my bones trying to grind me to a halt.

It was nothing I did; it was not in the way I acted or communicated; it was not who I was, but who I'd brought with me into this life.

My knees buckle, one fails completely, driving me into the sand, but I drag myself along on one knee, pulling with my hands. The boy slows, looks down at me. He says nothing, does nothing to help.

Take him with you, wherever it is that you're going. Take him from us.

I fall forward onto one shoulder, lurch ahead another few inches, handfuls of sand gripped tightly, eyes shut against the sun's brilliant reflection. This didn't used to affect me. I was meant for this. This is *mine.*

I crumple in the sand on my side, panting, my lungs feeling like they've been punctured with glass.

The boy, still standing a few feet ahead of me, walks a couple of steps closer, and just looks down at me, a certain childlike pity in his eyes. "Now it is mine," he says, and stands up.

As sand blows around me, filling the crevasses between my body and the ground, tucking me in for the storm to come, the stranger in the wide-brimmed hat does not say any final words in my head, does not appear one last time, squatting nearby, holding his sword in his lap, his face hidden from all light.

He does not give me a reason for any of this.

The boy turns, puts one foot in front of the other, and walks away from me.

I watch him go, more sand piling around me.

Though I am no longer capable of turning my head to look behind me, there is no need to. I feel the black curtain that has followed me my entire life swallow the light of the sun, an immense shadow dropping to earth.

As my own world turns dark, I see through squinted, sand-blown eyes as the boy disappears into the bright day ahead.

Walking.

The sun beating his back like a fist.

DEAD ANNIE'S SONG

Seth Lindberg

Louisville. Four nights and three shows in the dead heat of summer. Dashiell had never been to Louisville, and, upon arrival, immediately wanted to leave. The city was filled with a kind of self-conscious redneck hipster you could only really find in a state like Kentucky.

They slept in the van, with their gear.

The first night went well, until the sound system kicked out entirely. Dashiell was in the middle of singing the bridge for "Dead Annie's Song" and kept singing and playing for five seconds or more, thinking the sound'd come back in. They'd stood on the stage for another ten minutes watching an already bored audience grow restless and irritated.

The promoter felt bad, and after the set bought them drinks.

The second night Bear requested they take "Dead Annie's Song" out of the setup. Bad luck, he muttered. Hesitantly the rest of the band agreed.

"Well, what'll we replace it with?" asked Dashiell. "Dead Annie's Song" was his favorite. It had taken him a month to work it over, fixing the chorus and letting the chord progressions flow smoothly. Their sole quiet song, with a simple bassline and the rainlike patter of the drums, building up to its self-destructive finale. The song was as close to cartharsis as Dashiell got. It irritated him to not play it.

"We could do 'Eleanor Rigby'," Stull offered. Stull and Bear had worked on that one as a lark. Sometimes they played the Beatles' song to warm up.

"No way. No covers," Dashiell said.

"Oh, come on. All starting bands do covers. It gives the audience something to—"

Dashiell frowned. "We've gone over this. Do we get known for clever covers or for our *own* stuff?"

Bear grumbled, shifting his large frame.

Trace spoke up, pushing a shock of faded green hair out of her face. "So we just end it early, then?" Her tone expressed disapproval.

"Well," said Dashiell, hesitantly.

"Come on, Dash," said Stull. "It'll be fun."

Bear stroked his beard. "Do you want to do it, Trace?"

Trace shrugged, glancing at Dashiell. "Sure, we need another song." She flashed him a guilty look.

"That makes three votes, Dashiell," said Bear. "We play it."

Dashiell sighed, his shoulders slumping. "All right."

They played in a cramped bar near Seton College with two local bands. The first band had a girl singing blandly backed up by two guys, one on string bass and the other on drums. They were met by polite applause.

Bear and Stull drank the whole time. Dashiell fidgeted nervously, watching the crowd.

"It's gonna be all right," said Trace as the second band set up.

The new guys looked like outcasts from the dimension of Britpop. They had shaggy, teased hair and wore shiny shirts and tight pants. Within minutes they were playing loudly.

"Yeah, I know," said Dashiell, the delay in his response making him feel awkward. He didn't look at her. "Do you think we'll ever grow out of this?" He motioned to the stage.

"Grow out of playing music? I hope not."

"No . . ." He shook his head. "Grow out of these small clubs.

"Oh," she said. Her voice grew distant. "I don't know. Aren't we . . . I mean, the music, that's the important thing. That we're making music." She didn't sound confident.

Dashiell wanted to die. The Britpop exiles were about to leave the stage.

Bear put a massive hand on his shoulder. "Come on," he said. "We're going to do a shot of Jaeger before we hit the stage."

"Why not?" he said.

They opened with "Three Fists," a loud, fast song with a heavy bassline. The song required Dashiell and Stull to sync up the chord progression for the chorus, and by the second one Dashiell realized he'd fallen in a half beat off. He let Stull raggedly lead them through the song while he choked out the lyrics and mentally cursed himself. He'd played the song a million times. He knew it better than this.

The next few songs didn't fare any better, but no worse either. Dashiell couldn't get into the rhythm: he felt conscious of his playing, and conscious of the band. The lyrics stumbled out, but he didn't care. They probably couldn't hear him over the distortion anyway.

The audience sat watching him, all expectant faces. The Britpop refugees and their girlfriends took up the majority of the seats, holding court to one side of the stage. Bile welled up in the back of Dashiell's throat.

The band murdered their way through the set. No one danced, no one's expressions changed. The audience respectfully clapped when the band paused for a break, and usually Dashiell wouldn't let them, pushing them into another song as fast as the old one ended. He wouldn't take their false applause. He didn't need it, or so he tried to prove.

He let his eyes go unfocused, singing "Shame You," trying to banish the audience from his mind. He sung to the ceiling or to God, his eyes staring upwards. As the song hit the last chorus he felt in the moment, either finally lost to the music or drunk at last.

He opened his eyes, and forced himself to look at the audience. To play for them, the undeserving bastards, to give his heart and anything else he could push at them, assault them with his very soul. His eyes searched their passive faces as the music crescendoed, as Stull stomped on his pedal and feedback and noise washed over the tiny club.

That's when he saw her, the girl in blue. That was the first time.

Eyes. Dark blue eyes full of need and grief. Her face pale, roundish, soft, framed by jet black hair, the tattered sky-blue coat over a darker shade dress.

She stunned him, somehow, but his body was on autopilot, the words coming out without any change of intensity. He recovered, staring back at her, losing the rest of the audience, playing just for her, focusing on her like she was some kind of spiritual anchor for him. And maybe it was just his imagination but he could almost see her parting her lips, trying to mouth the words in time with his shattered lyrics.

He cut right over the slower grind of "I Was Waiting" and played those choppy first few chords of "This Machine"—the band didn't pick up at first but Stull's guitar kicked in loudly, playing like he was on fire and the rhythm just had to follow. And by the second refrain the band played as one, fast and loud and completely without apology.

When the set ended, the crowd fell into scattered applause. Cheers from the Britpop band, who grinned and waved enthusiastically. He smiled fiercely, feeling like victory pulled from the jaws of defeat. He glanced first at Stull, who looked strangely disappointed, like a charging dog feeling the pull of his leash. To his left Trace was already unslinging her bass, beads of sweat on her forehead.

Dashiell turned back to the crowd and quickly looked through the audience, searching for the girl, but couldn't find her. *Probably already left,* he thought to himself. *I could throw off my guitar and run out into the parking lot . . . but, but that would just be dramatic.*

The Britpop band came over, all grins and teased hair. "Great stuff," the first one drawled. "'Specially right at the end."

"Yeah," his compatriot added, all smiles. "And 'Eleanor Rigby.' Eleanor-fucking-Rigby. Never thought that song could be played fast, or without fucking cellos. Brilliant!""

Stull had a victorious grin. Dashiell tried to ignore him. "Thanks," he mumbled, looking as honest as he could, then politely excused himself for a drink.

Two days later they were in Lexington, playing in a hall rented from the Veterans of Foreign Wars with two bands made up of kids from local high schools. The first band seemed to have something against their instruments entirely. The lead singer shrieked off-key while the other three boys grimly tried to keep up. The drummer lost one of his sticks. Guitar strings kept snapping as they played on.

The scattering of friends, chaperones, and smiling parents looked on politely. The hall could have easily fit five hundred. Perhaps forty stood on the grey Formica tiles. They all kept their heads cocked to one side with sedate, yet baffled grins, looking like a herd of confused cattle.

The popular kids were all outside, drinking smuggled alcohol and engaging in complex mating rituals like one would find about lemurs on the Learning Channel. Dashiell had wanted to watch the show but got sick of kids trying to buy pot from him. He found his compatriots out by the van, smoking cigarettes and guarding the equipment.

Trace sat on the bumper of the van, fuming. "I thought you said this was some kind of punk thing," she snarled.

"I thought it was," Stull replied, sounding six kinds of defensive. He lifted his cigarette up to his mouth and inhaled. "The kid on the phone made it out to be something almost rave-like."

"A rave? A fucking *rave*?" Trace looked incredulous. "Oh my god, that would have been even worse."

"Well, a punk rave," said Stull, his voice small.

"A punk rave," said Trace. "Jesus-*fucking*-Christ."

"I think," said Bear slowly, "this is some kind of . . . high school dance." Trace just rolled her eyes.

"The kid on the phone just said . . . he said it would be this underground thing," Stull muttered. "Like, some festival."

"We've been had." Trace sighed.

They stood there in the humid Kentucky night, no one bothering to speak.

She was there, though. Halfway through the set he saw her. Angry and hurt, a vintage hat on her head. Blue hair. Blue dress. Blue hat. Stark eyes, lipstick a red washed to black with the lighting.

They were playing one of their worst sets. Not like it mattered. The forty teens in the audience were too interested in one another, and their chaperones probably liked Credence and the Eagles.

He looked right at her, playing to her, playing through her. "Call for Clouds" ended in its usual uncomfortable way, rumbling to a halt like a car that had just lost its breaks. He glanced quickly at Stull and Trace. Trace was beginning to show signs of tiring, while Stull looked like he was just starting to find his rhythm for the night. Stull played out the end of "Call for Clouds" a few minutes later than normal, then glanced quickly down at the set list. Dashiell could see him grin. "Three Fists" was next. Stull's favorite.

Dashiell usually wrote lyrics first, then found a good melody to frame it with. After the framework of the song was created, he would show it to the band, who would tool around with various ideas. Trace would get her bassline down, then usually run off to her boyfriend of the time.

Then Stull would tear the thing apart and piece it back together, leaving Dashiell with a wounded ego and all the best melodic ideas gone. But the night he brought over "Three Fists," Stull was already drunk. Bear knew why, but he refused to tell it to Trace or Dash. So, with reservations, they played on. When Dashiell got to his raw, loud, new song he had written in a pique of frustration, lyrics still incoherent but the melody all there, Stull took to it like a sailboat to wind.

It was their best collaboration outside of "Dead Annie's Song," a song they fought over constantly, bringing out the best and worst of each other. With that song, Stull was uncompromising with Dashiell. He wouldn't accept anything he thought was lacking. Nothing but the best would do.

"I just wish you wouldn't be so harsh," Dashiell told him once.

"I'm harsh because of how brilliant it might be," Stull replied.

Dashiell saw Stull's grin and turned to speak the first few lines: "We could have been/we could have been/we could have . . ." And then, perfectly timed, the four brought their instruments to the song, and the song raged through them as one, hurtling through the hall. He could feel tears in his eyes as he looked up, seaching the girl out.

She was gone. She never existed. The teens continued to stare up at the stage, impassively.

Their set ended a bit too short. Dashiell didn't care, he knew the others felt the same way. He rushed out to find the girl, weaving through the crowd. She was nowhere, his girl in blue.

He passed by two kids loitering near the bathrooms. Neither saw him. "What'd you think of the set?" asked one.

"You mean the headliners?"

"Yeah."

"They were all right, I guess."

"Yeah, I wasn't that impressed neither. I liked that 'Eleanor Rigby' song, though."

"Who did that? Some British band, right?"

"Yeah, I think Oasis."

Dashiell quietly walked off, his fists clenched and his face flushed.

* * *

Back in Cincinnati, the gigs started spreading themselves out a little more than they were used to. Dashiell got a job painting houses with a friend from high school. Working outside in the hot humid Ohio-valley summers wasn't his idea of a great job, but he found the job peaceful after a while. You could spend hours painting the side of the house, completely lose track of time, lose track of yourself.

He'd come home, spend an hour in front of his keyboard trying to pound lyrics out or on his guitar, practicing chords. Then give up, play video games.

They still practiced "Dead Annie's Song"—Dashiell and Stull wouldn't have it any other way. But none of the four (outside of Dashiell, that is) wanted to play it live.

"Bad luck," Bear said dismissively, when Dashiell brought it up.

"What do you mean by that?"

Bear growled. "We'll get halfway through the song, and something will break. A wire will short. An amplifier give out, a string break—on Stull's guitar. Stull, of all people. Remember last spring, our gig at the Rusty Nail, I had a cymbal crack on that song. A cymbal. You know how hard it is to break that? That thing's metal."

"You don't know it was during that song."

"I do. It had to be. It sounded different after that. I know my set, Dash."

"We'll play it one more time."

"No, we won't. We can't afford it."

"It's our best song!"

"It is. And it'll be great when we make that demo we keep planning on recording. But we can't play it live."

Dashiell looked over to Trace, but she shrugged, uncaring. Stull flashed him a guilty look, then glanced away.

Three shows in two weeks, and the mystery girl in blue showed up to each one. Each time, a look of pain on her face, getting worse in time. Worse with each passing moment. Worse with each new song.

The local crowds in Cincinnati waxed and waned, depending

on the season. Summers could be dry for local bands, when most of the students from the U. of Cincinnati and Xavier University were back home. The band had a following, however small. Friends, partiers, people who liked their music loud and fast and meaningful and complicated and moody. Guys in faded Metallica shirts next to hipsters wearing beige with goatees. They sweated through the hot, humid nights to shake their fists in time with music.

Some measure of success, but not enough for Dash or Stull. There had to be a better way of getting more people to their shows, but nothing seemed to work.

And the girl, the nameless girl, she mystified him. She began to invade his dreams, though always remained silent.

A month later, she spoke to him.

It was down on that Laundromat/club on Compton, just across from Bogart's and two blocks away from the university. A local play-off between two bands from Dayton and two from Cincinnati was happening—something done a few months back at another club that turned out to be massively successful for all parties involved. Tonight, an A&R man was supposedly in attendance, but no one could see a suit in the entire place.

They played third in the set by luck of the draw, invited in by friends of theirs, a Dayton punk band called Crucial Matter that they met at Wright State, then toured some clubs with on the OSU campus up in Columbus, after that hit some clubs a month later in Cleveland and Akron. Good guys, kids, though. Hyper. They had a fan base of their teenaged girlfriends and accumulated friends, but they could only show up to all-ages shows.

Bear and Trace stood near the front to cheer the Crucial kids on. Stull was in the back, warming up like a boxer preparing for a big fight—pacing around like a leashed animal, baring his teeth. It was either that or booze for Stull. Booze to calm him down, bring him back to earth, but that seemed like a bad habit to get started on.

Dashiell had bought his traditional bourbon-and-Coke and

found a place off to the side where he could perch on a stool and remain relatively unnoticed. He liked to watch the bands work the crowd, and he liked to watch the crowd itself. It took a particular vantage point to be able to really observe both.

Crucial Matter played an emotional set, though not terribly technically proficient. Their sole recognizable song, "Slack Attack," drew some response, though only when Bear and Trace started to chant along with the chorus from the sidelines.

He sensed someone there, next to him, and wondered how long that person had been standing next to him. It could have been for several songs. He turned his head to get a good corner-of-the-eye look at who it might be.

The girl. He recognized her, even though he'd never seen her profile before. She had a good profile, a worthy one. Enough of a chin to keep it from being weak, not too much to look awkward. High cheekbones, small nose. Large eyes shaded by dark blue eyeshadow.

His heart leapt to his throat. He suddenly lost any idea of what to say. She watched Crucial Matter confer with each other on the tiny stage.

"Having fun?" he croaked, lamely.

Her eyes darted over to him, then back. "Oh," she said, boredly, "I'm just waiting." Her voice had that slow Southern accent of a ladylike woman who just can't seem to care.

"For what?"

She turned to look at him, three-fourths profile. Faint tendrils of a smile on her bow-shaped lips. "Why," she started innocently, "for my favorite band, of course."

His heart raced in his chest, but he had no idea why. Two bands after Crucial Matter—one of them his. "Which one?"

"You should know," she said, slyly.

A pause. The band on stage started again. After a moment, he shouted at her, "What's your name?"

"Guess!" she called back.

He really had no idea. A thought came to his head. "Is it Annie?" Annie. Dead Annie's Song. Perhaps he'd somehow conjured her when making that terribly sad melody. A wrathful spirit, angry at being awakened, wrecking the band when they played it live, but waiting for it when they didn't, trapped, trapped like he was . . .

It all fit like jigsaw. Click click click, all the pieces put together.

"Annie?" Her brow furrowed in confusion.

"No, guess again . . . " she called back, sounding disappointed in him.

"I really don't know, then," he replied.

"You don't?" She laughed, shrilly, barely heard over the cacophony from the speakers. "Your loss, then, Dashiell." She turned and walked away, her hips swaying slightly as she moved past someone.

She knows my name, he thought. He felt a little more than worried. Where did he know her from? Was she somehow stalking him? How did she fade in and out of crowds so quickly, then?

Crucial Matter's set came to a cluttered finale. After the cheers ended, Cody, the lead singer came over to him.

"Yo, man," said Cody.

Dashiell looked up. "Hey, what's up?"

"Nothin'." Cody grinned.

"Good set, by the way. "Slack Attack" rocked."

Cody brightened. "Really? Wow, thanks! So, who was that chick I saw you with?"

Wow, he thought. He saw her, too. "I didn't get her name."

Cody shook his head. "Fuckin' shame, man. What a hottie. Blue hair. Very cute!" He spoke like that, in quick fragments. It crept into his lyrics, too.

Dashiell grinned. "She was, wasn't she?"

"Heh. You better watch yourself. Chick like that. Rip you apart!" Cody laughed.

They played a shorter set than usual—just four songs, the penalty for trying to cram in all the bands in one night. Dashiell hit the stage somehow terrified that something was out of his control;

the band would be out of sync with one another, that Trace would forget the bridge to "Shame You," that someone's instrument would break, that his voice would choke. A thousand frights. But, of course, none of them would necessarily come true. They weren't playing "Dead Annie's Song" tonight, after all.

How did that work, to create a song that was cursed? What went in to that? It didn't feel any different in making it, it was just a little harder to get down right, put under a little more scrutiny than usual. But not even enough revision to mention.

He talked to the mystery girl tonight, but felt as confused as ever about her. It made him feel a little like tempting fate. With the rest of the band, he slung on his guitar, plugged it into the amplifier, and did a few quick tests. He looked up to watch Trace stand up to the stage, watching the audience chattering happily with itself, testing out the microphones.

He played a stripped-down version of the chord progression of the song. No one noticed, save Stull, who turned around and quirked an eyebrow. Dashiell could barely see him with the club's lights shining behind him. He gave Stull a helpless smile in response, and stopped playing.

Stop tempting Fate, he thought. He gazed out at the crowd, looking for his nameless girl. Waiting for approval.

Stull walked up to him. He towered over Dashiell, a sharp silhouette in the glare of the lights. "Y'ready?" Stull huskily asked. He bounced on the balls of his feet.

Dashiell craned his neck to look around Stull. He couldn't spot the girl.

"Sure, yeah," Dashiell said.

Stull grinned like a skull. "Great." He turned to the audience, testing a melody on his guitar. Stull's intensity was contagious.

Dashiell checked the strap of his guitar, then the plug to the amplifier. He rose, and walked to the center. The babble from the audience died down, expectantly. He felt like Ceaser addressing his legions.

He glanced down at the setlist, then at Trace and Stull. Trace looked nervous, which made her look ill in turn. Stull just grinned at him again. The first song, "This Machine," started off with their Big Black ripoff: Dashiell's guitar screaming like a shattered leg for a few bars, then the rest of the band hits in at the same time, pounding bass, drums, and two howling guitars.

A few people, drunk or charged up from the first two acts, began dancing or swaying. But the rest stood and watched. The crowd resisted, and the band fought harder.

Two songs later, playing their best and hardest, and the crowd seemed hardly moved at all. Stull seemed angry, Dashiell felt tense, Trace uncomfortable, and Bear as passive as always.

Fourth song: "Eleanor Rigby," and the audience began to cheer, erupt in surprise. Dashiell flushed, furiously, losing tempo. He sang the song through his teeth, ashamed. The crowd loved it.

Two songs to go, and they tried to carry the energy from the cover into their next. Dashiell scanned the audience, looking for the girl in blue. He couldn't find her, but his eyes lit on Trace's boyfriend, who raised his fist and shouted something at Dashiell as encouraging as it was unintelligible.

Their last song. "Three Fists." Stull's favorite. They played around with it tonight, starting with Stull's guitar and letting the rest catch up. Dashiell howled the song, going hoarse as he did, glaring at the audience. They'd opened up, a little. He could see bobbing heads. It wasn't enough, damn it. He screamed through clenched teeth, frustrated, angry. The songs, endlessly revised, reworked, cut apart, put back together, and cut apart again. All the time spent, wasn't it enough? Slashing his skin and letting the blood drip into lyrics, and they still stood there so passive. Why? What would it take? What did he have to *do* to make them listen?

He could rip his heart out and give it to them, and the tiny morsel that each person in the crowd would get couldn't even begin to sate their appetites. He lowered his head, letting his sweat-drenched hair fall in his eyes.

He looked up, and she was there. In pain. In agony, actually. Did she share his frustration? Or did his passion, his songs tear her apart? He stared at her as he sang, horrified. Her face pulled back into a wince, eyes tightly shut, arcing her head back in a sickeningly erotic pose, tears falling from her eyes as she clenched shut her jaw. No one noticed, they all stood there, drinking beer, watching the band, someone dancing chaotically nearby.

She looked up, right at him, and smiled. He couldn't tell if it was the terrified, defiant grin of a mouse to a cat, or the cat's own playful reply.

They met the A&R man after the show. He looked like a frat boy, older than Dash and Trace by a few years, but younger than Bear or even Stull. He wore a Vandals tee shirt, and torn jeans, eighties-style. The Vandals weren't even on his label.

"You guys have energy," the A&R man said, "and a lot of talent. I'd give you a few years and I could see some major labels courting you."

Bear and Trace looked legitimately impressed. Stull's grin was more of the shit-eating variety, though. This was his third serious band. He had a biological imperative to succeed, and soon. His body wouldn't be able to handle a rock-star overdose for much longer.

"Oh, come on," said Dashiell, trying to sound like he was kidding. "You don't think we're ready now?"

The A&R man sniffed a bit. "Your songs are certainly eager, but they're a little sloppy. You don't know how to end the things, either. They just sort of sputter to a close, or they rush too quickly to an end. If you worked on your endings a little, you could have some good songs."

Three weeks later, the day of a friend's party, they practiced for six hours straight. It was one of those rare Saturdays everyone had free. A week straight of rushing to finish painting a three-story Victorian up in the suburb of Wyoming, Ohio, and Dashiell was too tired to hold down on the frets of his guitar correctly.

"What about our endings?" Trace asked, for about the fiftieth time that day. "I think we need to work on them."

"I don't," Stull said, flatly.

"Christ," breathed Bear, half to himself.

Trace shot Dashiell a helpless look. He really didn't know what to think anymore. He just wanted it to end. "She might have a point," he muttered, defeated. Meaning, not Trace, but the A&R man. Stull glared at him. He knew what Dashiell meant.

"Thank you," Trace said, her voice like winter.

"How about this," said Dashiell. "We work on one song, fix it up a little, and see what goes there. Sound good?" He looked at Trace and Stull, hopefully.

Trace nodded. "Sure, I guess," Stull said, keeping his arms folded.

"All right, then," said Dashiell. "How about, ah, 'Call for Clouds'? I'm sure we can cut it down a bit."

"Sure," said Trace.

"Whatever," said Stull.

Dashiell sighed. "Okay, then." He started playing out the intro to the song, ignoring the painful complaints of his fingers.

"One question?" said Bear.

The three turned to look at him. Bear sat behind the drumset, stroking his beard worriedly. "Will the drum parts change too much?"

"No!" they all said, in unison, though each for their own reasons.

That night they all hit the party. They drank, they caught up with old friends. The party got crowded, so Dashiell sat out on the roof, drinking beer from the keg in his plastic cup. Eventually most of the roof inhabitants ended up back inside. Even at night, the Cincinnati summer was oppressively hot. It was something you got used to, though, when you worked outside.

About when he started to feel the beer hit him, he realized who was next to him. "Hey," he said.

"Hey," she drawled back, her voice still just too Southern to care.

"Nice night," he said absently. "Almost peaceful."

"I guess," she replied.

He didn't respond. He watched the heat ripple the streetlights for a few moments, and drank his beer.

"Do you know who I am, yet?" she asked. He couldn't tell if there was hope in her voice.

"Not a clue," he said, affecting an air of boredom. What did it matter, anyway? His band was going nowhere, almost breaking up. His songs, his life . . . *certainly eager, but a little sloppy.* He'd put everything into this band. If he didn't have that, what was he? Some house painter?

He heard a strange sound from her, and she looked away, her blue hair falling in her face. "I should go," she choked.

He reached for her arm. She felt cold. Cold and lifeless. "Wait," he said.

She turned to look at him. Her eyes looked only pale in the darkness, though welled up with tears. He moved his head closer, staring at her eyes. His nose brushed hers. She didn't pull back.

What the hell, he thought, and kissed her.

She let him, at first, then finally kissed back urgently, pressing her body against his. He traced the musculature of her back with his hand. They spent the rest of the night like that, locked, while the party babbled on through the window.

"You know why the French call it a little death," she said as she straddled him later that night. "They say with each time, the woman pulls a bit of the man's life out of him. With each time, a part of him dies." Her voice was husky and low.

He looked up at her and smiled.

"So, Dashiell. How may times do you want to die tonight?"

* * *

Trace was the first to notice it. "You've changed," she said, furrowing her brow and putting a hand on her hip.

Dashiell rubbed his temples. His splitting headache wasn't getting any better. "What are you talking about?"

"I don't know. You look different."

"Whatever. Let's play through the new ending again."

* * *

"So, what's your name?" he asked her one night. Friends had surprised him a visit, but somehow she knew to wait until they left. It was two in the morning. He had to get up at six to get to work.

"Oh," she said, "I'm no one."

"That's an odd name."

"I'm an odd girl."

* * *

Three shows later, and each one worse than the other. It seemed hardly worth it anymore. Could be a long time until they get another break. The college scene was getting old. And each time, the girl in blue, his No One, seemed to be in more pain than the last. After each time, she seemed more hollow, more weak.

"We need another little tour," Stull kept saying. Nobody could make time off of work.

They ended up at another club with Crucial Matter. Cody ran up after the set. "Great show!"

"Thanks, same with you."

"So. You know. Up in Dayton? Some friends, they have . . ." He waved, airily. "A label. Nothing big! But I said you rocked. Feel like a trip sometime?"

"Sure. Talk to Stull, though, okay?"

"Hey! No prob. You kicked tonight! Really!"

"You too, Cody."

* * *

The nights were amazing, but left him worn out. "I love you," he told her between deaths one night.

"You would," she replied ruefully.

* * *

They decided on another tour, covering the whole of the southern Ohio, up through Dayton and Miami, up to Columbus, then over to Marietta, then back again to Cincinnati. They packed everything in Stull's van.

"You should eat something," Bear told him on the ride up to their first gig.

Dashiell glanced over. "I'm fine."

"You should, you're so thin these days."

"I'm fine."

Stull glanced back from the driver's seat. "Stop mothering him, Bear," he said, sharply.

Bear just rumbled, and shared a look with Trace.

They played an amazing set at the all-ages show up in Dayton. Cody and Crucial Matter brought out all their friends, ready for a good time and primed to go. He spotted her during "I Was Waiting" in the back, her looks washed out in the lights to blacks and greys. She kept her searching eyes on him, her brow furrowed and her lips pursed. Towards the end, she coughed and choked, and some black liquid dripped out of her mouth. She just watched him, oblivious. By the next song, she was gone.

Cody's friends spoke like him. The label 'executive' hadn't even finished high school, but the band listened to him and ended up impressed with his knowledge. They'd have to come up with costs for studio time, but the kids were willing to throw an impressive amount of money at them, for, well, high school kids.

He caught a glimpse of her at the motel when he went out for ice. He followed her out to the parking lot. She fell into his arms.

"You're dying," he said, as she held him. She still felt cold.

"Am I?" she asked.

He growled, frustrated. "Why can't you ever tell me anything? Why can't you be straight for me, just once? What the hell is happening to you? What can I do to help? What the hell do you *want*?" He realized he was shaking her, and stopped, but still held on to her shoulders.

She lifted her chin to face him, and gave him an ancient look. "I want you to release me."

"How?"

"If I could tell you how, you would have done it by now," she said. "Now, do you want to die tonight, or what?"

He blinked. "Out here in the parking lot?"

She gave him a smile of mischief painted over exhaustion. "Where else?"

She looked stiffened at the Miami show, and afterwards, when he saw her, she looked as if her skin had tightened on her considerably. He wanted to walk up to her, but someone came up to congratulate him on his night's performance. He said thanks. It wasn't a great show. The crowd never really got into it. They rarely do for bands like theirs, it seemed.

In Columbus she wore a blue plastic low-cut dress that accented what little cleavage she had left. The tears she cried were blood that night. They dripped black down her face, collecting obscenely between her breasts.

The night before the Marietta show, they drifted into town, staying at a motel on the outskirts. Trace was up half the night on the phone with her boyfriend. The boys left to hang out at a bar, when they came back, she was still on the phone, crying. She hung up soon after, but refused to talk about it.

They went out for more booze, drank solemnly in the motel room. Dashiell kept finding excuses to leave, but his girl in blue wasn't in the parking lot, was nowhere to be found.

He returned to find everyone fairly drunk. Trace finally stood up, a little wobbly. "I have an announcement to make," she said, solemnly.

"What is it?" Stull asked.

"I'm quitting the band." She looked at Dashiell, then looked away.

"What?" said Bear, confused.

"You can't!" said Stull.

"Why?" said Dashiell.

She shook her head. "We're being pulled apart here, and I hate watching it. We had our good times, but they're over. It was a good try. We could have made something. But it's not going to happen."

"No," said Stull. "It *is* going to happen."

Trace folded her arms. "My boyfriend wants to break up with me. He says I spend too much time with the band. He gave me an ultimatum tonight. Him or you. I'm . . . I'm sorry." She started crying. "I love him."

Dashiell had never heard her say that before. His thoughts were interrupted by Stull's voice: "You're going to break up the band over some stupid guy? What the hell is wrong with you?"

Trace's pain turned to anger. "What the hell is wrong with *you*, Stull? Have you really looked at Dash recently? He's practically rotting away! But nobody's allowed to say anything about it without you getting all huffy about how fine he is. Fuck that. You're a bastard, Stull! I'm sick of you!" She stalked out of the hotel room, slamming the door behind her.

Dashiell blinked. "I'm . . . I'm fine!"

Stull looked shocked. He didn't say anything. He wouldn't meet Dashiell's eyes.

"Uh, someone should go after her, probably," Bear said, uncomfortably.

Stull nodded. "You go," he said.

Bear grunted and walked out.

Stull looked up at Dashiell. "You dying on me?"

Dashiell shook his head. "No. No, I'm not."

Stull watched him for a moment, not saying anything. "I believe you. Do you believe me that I . . . " He shook his head. "Fuck it. You need a drink?"

"Yes. I think I do."

"Me too."

They played their last night in Marietta, or it was supposed to be their last night. Hardly anyone showed up. He looked for the girl in blue as he played. It seemed like his only reason to play, but she toyed with him, finally appearing at the end, but only briefly, a shadow of herself, hugging herself tightly, her eyes shrouded by her ragged bangs. No one noticed her.

"We'll find another bassist," Stull kept saying. Dashiell looked at Bear. Bear didn't try to hide his look. He was leaving, too.

Some end to their great band. Like their songs, it all sort of fizzled out, unfocused. It struck Dashiell as terribly ironic. Even in their career, they couldn't get the endings right.

They drove back to Cincinnati in silence. Hours of riding, watching scenery go by. They didn't even play music. No one could muster up the energy to pick something.

He lay in the back, wrapping himself with a spare blanket. What am I going to do with myself now? he wondered. Do I start a new band with Stull? Do I quit entirely? Do I get a real job? What happens to all these songs? Will they ever get played again? Was all this effort for nothing?

None of his questions left him with any answers.

The night he returned, she showed up on his doorstep at four in the morning. Her hair looked ragged and tossed, her eyeliner smeared so much she looked like a raccoon.

"Oh, it's no one," he said.

"Fuck you," she spat, and pushed her way into the house. He blinked, watching her. "I hate you, I hate you, I hate you. How could you let me suffer like this, you bastard!"

He blinked, speechless.

She turned, fixated on his expression, and leapt at him, scratching his face with her nails, trying to gouge out his eyes or claw at his face. The first hit stung, then he threw his arms up, tossing her back with surprising ease. She stayed on the floor, curling up and sobbing.

He stepped over to her, gingerly, and put an arm around her. "It's because of the band, isn't it?" he asked, softly.

She stopped her sobbing only long enough to say, "You idiot."

"I'll get together the band. Once last time. They will for me. I'll play you that song. I'll play "Dead Annie's Song" for you. Will that do it? Will that stop your suffering?"

She stopped her sobbing, and looked up at him out of the corner of her eye. "If you play that song," she said, carefully, "play it for yourself." But she seemed calmer than before.

It was easy to organize. One last hurrah for the kids. Stull agreed immediately, Bear wasn't long behind. Trace took a bit more convincing, but she agreed to do it 'for him.' Dashiell called down to Lexington and got those killer Britpop exiles to come north, and of course, Crucial Matter to come down from Dayton for one last bit of 'rivalry.'

They played to a packed club full of rowdy students returning from summer break. The Britpop exiles played a mean set; better than they'd been the first time they'd played with him by quite a bit. Crucial Matter was all over the place, but from the way they were acting, it very well might have been the first time the band had ever gotten drunk.

They fought over the set list, one last time. "I'm taking "Eleanor Rigby" out," said Dashiell.

"You can't do that," said Stull, "It's now our signature song!"

Dashiell winced. "I can. It's not ours."

"Aw, but everyone likes it," said Bear.

"I'm with Dash," said Trace. "It's just not 'us'."

Stull folded his arms. "We should play it. They're expecting it."

Dashiell bit his lip, angrily. "That song is cursed!" he blurted out.

Stull and Bear both blinked. "What? How?"

"It just is," said Dashiell, testily. "We play 'Dead Annie's Song' instead."

"But that one is, too!" said Bear, sounding half his age.

"It's our last night. And it's our best song. What can possibly happen?"

Bear looked up dubiously.

"'Three Fists' is our best song," mumbled Stull.

Dashiell sighed, testily. "Well, okay. Outside of 'Three Fists,' it's our best song. So, are we playing it?"

"Yeah."

"Sure."

"Great!"

They played that night, hard and loud. The songs flowed quickly to one another. The crowd was lively and on their side—filled with all sorts of familiar faces, friends of theirs, co-workers, people in other local bands they played with or shared practice spaces, some people who actually went to every local show they ever did. Some people even knew a few of the lyrics to the songs, and shouted them out. They played off the crowd, and the crowd played off of them. It was great. It was everything that playing live was supposed to be.

Until he saw the girl in blue, looking at him with eyes of need. Pain wracked her face, he could almost feel the pain sympathetically himself. But her song would have to wait.

They ended their set with the newly redone "Call for Clouds." The ending felt right, it resonated after the set ended, buoyed up by the cheers from the crowd. They took a short break, while people called for encores. Their first ever. First and last.

Dashiell found himself trembling at the end of the set. He felt so giddy with the energy of it all, it was hard for him to stand up.

Trace suddenly turned to him, eyes all concern. "Whoa, Dash. You all right?"

"Huh? I'm fine!"

Bear moved to support him. What was the big deal? He felt annoyed having the larger man prop him up. He just got a bit excited.

Stull came back, a head cocked to hear the cheering. He strode as if he was on top of the world, but he raised an eyebrow when he spotted Bear and Dashiell. "You guys up for an encore?" he asked, looking at Dashiell.

"Yeah, let's get 'em," Dashiell replied.

They barreled through "Three Fists," as people started to break out into applause and hoots and shouts. Their timing wasn't bad.

The sound system sucked. Nobody cared. He could hear people chanting along with the chorus, felt lifted by it, felt some tiny affirmation. His chorus. His lyrics.

They let it end, just barely, though Stull played with feedback while people from the audience jumped up, clapping and cheering and raising beer bottles to toast them. He could feel his heart racing. This was it. The cursed song.

What makes a cursed song, anyway? How the hell does it happen? Why, why does this beautiful and tragic little poem cause so much misfortune? He swallowed, getting ready to step back to the mic. He glanced at Stull, who nodded at him. Glanced at Trace, who was shooting him nervous looks. This song is for no one. It sounded weird. Would she get it? Would she understand? Would that be what it took to set her free?

He'd never understand what bound things to people. Perhaps never would. What bound her to him, what bound pain to some sad song he wrote about someone he'd never met.

"This song is . . . " For no one. That's what he wanted to say. For the girl who is not Dead Annie and this is not her song. This song is for everything tied to us, especially the things we can never understand. This song is for all the cursed songs and all the cursed songwriters. This song is for . . .

Of course. "This song is for Eleanor," he said, searching her out in the crowd. He caught her eye. She smiled. Who's to say his song was the first cursed song? In all likelihood, this has been going on since the beginning of time.

He started the song, that hollow minor chord progression, and the others joined in when they were supposed to. It played like a song that had rarely been played live. Not perfect. The band was a little off, here and there. But he sang with emotion, and he could feel them playing with emotion, too.

He could see his little blue-haired girl in the back of the club, staring at him. He could never guess what her looks meant, but he hoped that she wasn't in pain anymore. He caught her eye as the song crescendoed, and started to feel lightheaded. Then the song came down, loud and hard and full of fury, then ended on that note: "This is 'Dead Annie's Song' . . ." almost done, and nothing had broken, the lights hadn't gone out, none of the instruments had cracked or broken, and none of the band electrocuted. Amazing.

He hit the last note, and felt a little dizzy, and suddenly the stage was hurtling towards his head. He heard loud noises, and people talking, but it all sounded very distant. Oh well, he thought. Still cursed. Damn.

Someone was talking to him, but he couldn't hear what they were saying. He tried to recognize the faces around him, but they all just looked too . . . too many people. Where was Trace? Where was Stull? How about Cody?

Where was the A&R man, that fat little frat boy? He should have been here tonight, our crowning glory. And at the end of "Dead Annie's Song," he could have spat out "How's this for an ending, you bastard?" and toppled off like he did. It would have been perfect! He started laughing, which upset the muddled voices and faces.

He saw a figure in blue pushing through the crowd. She looked beautiful, even if it was hard to focus on her. Eleanor. She leaned down to kiss him, oblivious to figures crowding around him.

Her lips felt cold. She spoke two words and reached a small hand out to close his eyelids. Darkness.

THE COLLECTIVE

Brett Alexander Savory

Black dress shoes slapping wet concrete. A train whistle; gun shot; dog bark; police and ambulance sirens wailing. None of it registers. Only the slapping of the shoes on the pavement, and now the little white darts of hatred nestling, writhing, dreaming of release behind the eyes.

Brown eyes, blue eyes, green eyes, orange eyes, pink eyes—it does not matter. It is anonymous. Crimes perpetrated by The Collective.

And now there is a gun in my mouth.

I look up into the face that is attached to the neck that is attached to the shoulder that is attached to the arm that is outstretched and attached to the hand that holds the gun that is in my mouth. It is a fluid connection—one that I make in my mind over and again.

I blink sweat away; my forehead is a broken dam.

The man who holds the gun so steadily, unflinchingly in my mouth is no one I know, yet I know many people like him.

I have done bad things in my life. I have been alive twenty-seven years and I have done more than twenty-seven bad things. I have done more than twice that amount of bad things. I wonder if this man who holds the gun in my mouth knows about any of these things or if he just happened to randomly pick my sweating face to cram his weapon into.

Perhaps he does this every night of the week to someone different. Maybe he does not like his day job very much. Maybe someone there makes him feel out of control.

Staring into his eyes I can see that he does not recognize me; I can see that he does not hate *me* in particular, and that he has no idea about the far-more-than-twenty-seven bad things I have done in my life.

I think he hates doing what he is doing right now. I do not believe he enjoys holding guns in people's mouths. So I wonder what his motives are. I wonder why I am on my knees in a puddle in a basement garage next to my car, the keys still clenched in my hand, listening to the overhead broken water pipe dripping, listening to the police and ambulance sirens—the police who won't get here in time to stop this, and the ambulance that will be useless because of it.

This man is a member of The Collective. The Collective isn't dangerous; only its members are. You tend to think more about society's ills when you have a gun in your face.

When this man finally pulls the trigger, I know it will not hurt; there won't be enough time between the act of pulling the trigger and my death for there to be pain. So it is not pain that I am afraid of.

Since I have done awful things in my life—some worse than what this man is about to do—I know I have this coming to achieve at least partial balance in the cosmic scheme of things. I am not afraid of death. I think—now that I am down on my knees in a puddle waiting to die and have some time to reflect on it—that I have been waiting for it for many years.

What scares me is the fact that this man's face will not tell me why he's doing it. I am scared of not knowing why I'm going to die. If only there was a twitch in his cheek muscles, a shifting of his focus, something, anything to give me a clue . . . But there is nothing. He bores straight into my skull with his glare, and I can feel his pulse throbbing in a vein at the back of my head.

Maybe he does not know the exact things I have done, but I think he may know the kind of man that I am. I do not think I can hide that. I do not think any man can. You try to mask it, but some people see right through you, no matter what you do.

And really, I am very stupid—I should have seen this coming. Someone, somewhere is always watching you, and with a network as immense as The Collective, I do not know why I thought I would be different.

There is no such thing as a random act of violence.

I peeled the skin off a man's face once. It was not anything like peeling an orange. It was disgusting, but not disgusting enough that I didn't do it again to another man, in a different apartment. I told myself that he was enjoying it, that he was screaming with pleasure.

That was one of the bad things I did.

Another time, I thought about ramming my cock down my niece's throat. That felt worse than ripping off a man's face. That made me feel dirty on the inside as well as the outside.

So many things that I should not have done, and now I have a gun in my mouth. The man has cocked the weapon and is muttering something under his breath. I cannot make out what he is saying. Whatever it is, it must be about me. Everything is about me. I am the centre of my own, this man's, and everyone else's universe.

This is the way everybody thinks.

Time is slowing, winding down to the point where, when I lift my eyes to the dripping water pipe, I watch the droplets form and it seems to take an hour. Each one is one full hour, its descent is twice that, and when the third one finally hits the puddle beneath it, I hear the report of a gun. Suddenly I am lying on my back and I can feel that my face is gone. The man has pulled the trigger. I cannot see him anymore.

For a moment I wonder where he went. Then I hear his black dress shoes slapping the wet concrete, walking away.

The back of my head is opened up wide. The concrete is cool and makes me think of ice cream.

The man must have known those things I was thinking about my niece. If so, I wonder why he only shot me once.

Now I'm back on my knees, watching the ripples from the last drop of water edge out from the centre of the puddle. I blink sweat away and take a deep breath.

Not dead, just daydreaming.

I wonder what the man from The Collective will do with my corpse when he finally does pull the trigger. Is there a special cleanup crew that comes around to dispose of Those Who Could Not Be Collected?

Though I have done more than twenty-seven bad things in my life, I think, perhaps, this man has done more.

I would really like to scratch my chin. It is itchy. But I do not think the man will let me.

If I could do everything over again, I would do four times the bad things I've done. This man with the gun cannot change that, though I think maybe that is what he is trying to do. He thinks I will waste these final moments wishing I could take back those awful things. He does not know me as well as he thinks he does.

I would only like to take back one. And you already know what that is, so I won't say it again.

The itch under my chin is getting worse, and I am nearly to the point now where I might risk asking the man from The Collective if he wouldn't mind scratching it for me.

Drip-drip. Itch-itch. Insanity is repetition.

I'll bet he wants me to beg. That must be it. He is waiting for me to cry and grovel. He wants me to confess, come clean. Purge my soul before he stamps my ticket. God will forgive me for everything. Detail it all, lay it out in black and white, paint me a picture, spill your guts, let Jesus take the pain away, tell me how you love to watch people die, the lights winking out one by one by one by one in their eyes, so many lights, dampened, candles in the wind, and how you'd peel my skin off and boil it if I gave you half the chance, because oh, yes sir, most certainly I would, and how I thought about my cock in my niece's mouth, and how I need a shower, only the dirt never comes off when you think things like that, it sticks and makes you itch and itch and you can't scratch because you look up into the face that is attached to the neck that is attached to the shoulder that is attached to the arm that is outstretched and attached to the hand that holds the gun that is in your mouth.

It is a fluid connection—one that you make in your mind over and again.

But I will not confess.

Not to you, Jesus, or anyone else. What I have done is mine. The Collective cannot take it from me, even though I do not deserve to have it. I hold onto it because it defines me. Death has no scythe as long as I am defined.

We judge ourselves and live life accordingly, then let others clean up the mess. But the cleanup crew might miss a spot and I'll be forever imprinted, stained, given my own star on this cement walk of fame as the brightest and boldest of his era. A smudge will mark my place, and no one will ever know what I have done. My secret will become me.

So I hope the man from The Collective's purpose is not to make me confess, because if it is, I will be on my knees and he will be on his feet until we both ache in every muscle. He will wish he were home, reading the newspaper in a nice, soft chair; I will wish I had been the one who had made his chair for him, and who had written all the stories in the newspaper he was reading, created the ink the words were printed with, the paper they were written on.

I do not want to be a smudge. I want to redefine myself through this man. I want to become a part of his organization. I want to join the herd. If The Collective is every one of us, then I am already part of it; I am already doing what it wants me to. These thoughts are no longer my own, and I cannot know if they ever were.

I am a shiny star and I am about to die.

The man's trigger finger is perhaps as itchy as my chin now. My ears twitch and I hear the stiff, tiny tendons in his finger creak as he starts to gently squeeze the trigger.

And I know I said it before but there is no such thing as a

random act of violence. This is what I deserve. Twenty-seven times twenty-seven times twenty-seven times twenty-seven and I am judged. There is no way to take any of it back.

If I am—by my own will or not—part of The Collective, then this man should know my thoughts. So listen to me: my atrocities define me; your gun and your judgements cannot change that. I am exactly who you need me to be. Though you may deny it, you created me, so you are intrinsic to my definition.

The barrel of the gun slides backward; the sight gently knocks against my top row of teeth on its way out, and my mouth clicks shut.

The man walks away. Black dress shoes slapping wet concrete.

I stand up, listen to my knees snap and pop, blink once, and wipe at my forehead with my coat sleeve.

Feeling the keys in my hand, I open the driver's side door and get in. I turn the car on, flick on the windshield wipers and watch them for awhile, then drive home, counting to twenty-seven over and again until the numbers mean nothing, until the words that make up the numbers mean even less.

By the time I get home, I have forgotten what numbers and letters are altogether. I need a new way to communicate. I want to show The Collective that I understand. Now that I know the language of the organization, I am confident in my abilities to get my point across.

I am certain they will understand what I mean.

I walk in my front door, drop the keys on the hall table, go to the desk in my office, retrieve the pistol, sit in my office chair, review once again in my head exactly what is that I want to tell them, slide the barrel between my teeth.

And begin to speak.

•

SPIRITS OF ABSOLUTION

Seth Lindberg

Weave a circle round him thrice,
And close your eyes with holy dread,
For he on honey-dew hath fed,
And drunk the milk of Paradise.
—Samuel Taylor Coleridge, *Kubla Kahn*

"Y' scared?" she whispered. "You really are?"

* * *

Derek awoke feeling cramped, tired, and hung over. Pain shot through his legs. Daylight filtered in from somewhere in the compartment he rested in. He looked around, trying to shift his aching body into a more comfortable position. A crushed beer can dominated his view.

"Where am I?" he asked. More to himself than anyone.

He was answered with a grunt from somewhere, then a mumble. Derek rose, letting more beer cans cast off of him. He seemed to be in the backseat of a car, which in turn rested in a wooded grove. Everything stank of stale beer.

A figure rose up from the passenger seat. Long, half-dreaded hair tangled in his face. The hair was half-bleached and dyed a blue, which had rapidly faded to a teal color, like it'd spent too long in a chlorinated pool. "Where are we? Good question," the man rumbled. "Somewhere on our Quest."

"Quest?"

The man peered at him. "Wow, whatshername . . . " he rubbed his head. " . . . Melanie. Melanie really messed you up last night." He turned around slowly, "Where are the girls, anyway?"

Derek shrugged, "Beats me." Something about all this felt terribly wrong. He could readily imagine being here in this car, drinking, all of that. He couldn't put his finger on what, though. It's like it didn't add up.

He'd figure it out, sooner or later. He leaned back and tried to stretch his aching legs. "So what do we do now?" Might as well pretend to know the guy for now. Act like nothing's wrong.

"Don't know," the guy replied. "So, are you able to drive, you think?"

Good question, he thought. "I don't know. Probably need to stretch a bit."

"All right," the guy said, amiably. He suddenly chuckled, shaking his head. "Our parents are going to *kill* us."

Who are my parents, and why would they threaten to destroy me? he thought. The guy just seemed way too friendly about it all. Must be some figure of speech. Had to be.

They opened the car doors and stepped out. Birds sang merrily as the morning light filtered through the trees. Derek took a moment to stretch his legs. Looking down at his feet he noticed they were caked in dried mud. He reeked of stale beer.

"D'you know where they went?" the other guy asked.

Derek just grunted. He scanned the area. The clearing was desolate, removed from any sight or sound of human activity. Save, that is, for the car they were in.

"Fuck, where do you think they ran off to?"

Derek walked over to where the dirt road picked up. He kneeled down. "Home, I'm guessing."

"Huh?"

"Car tracks lead away. The girls took the other car," he reasoned, then added hesitantly, "right?" He looked back to scrutinize the other guy's expression.

His companion looked vague. "Right," he said after a moment. "I'm sorry. I guess I'm really not myself this morning, forgetting a simple thing like that."

Derek furrowed his brow. Maybe that's not all you've forgotten, he thought. He thought about admitting this amnesia to the man, or possibly catching him off guard, throwing him to the ground. Maybe he could put the man in a compromising position, twist an arm, get some information.

No, he thought. *I might need him later on. And as shaky as he's acting, he is my ticket back 'home.'* "Yeah," said Derek. "Well, maybe we should get home ourselves."

"Good idea." The other guy wandered around the car to slide into the driver's seat. Derek tried to hit some of the dirt off before he stepped back into the car. When he opened the passenger-side door, a few beer cans spilled out.

He glanced down at them for a moment. A part of him wanted to pick the cans up, put them back in the car. Not despoil the scenery. But that feeling came on him like some memory he couldn't understand.

He rubbed his face and stared out the passenger seat window as the car choked and sputtered to a start. His face and hair felt oily, almost crusted with dirt. The mild, throbbing pains on his hands and arms seemed to be tiny scratches, accompanied by one on his cheek.

He cautiously rubbed against one of the longer scratches on his arm. The wound was just beginning to scab up. With a bit of a pull, the scab came off with a bright twinge of pain. Dark red blood began to collect on his arm.

Interesting, he thought.

Derek wondered how much it might hurt if he cut deeper. Or took his whole hand off. He looked at his hand, imagined it severed and on his lap, his own dark blood pooling around him.

What it would be like to pick up one hand in the other, feel the dead flesh in fingers of one hand but not the other.

"Woah, Derek, you're bleeding," said the other guy. The car had found its way to a dirt road and made its way through the woods, kicking up a few clouds of dirt.

"Yeah," said Derek. It seemed like the right thing to say. I shouldn't cut off my hand, he thought. That'd probably annoy me after a while.

He could see a few uses for two hands. Suppose he needed to strangle someone to death? He couldn't very well do it one-handed. Maybe. But it'd be difficult, annoying, even. And drive a car—he probably wouldn't be able to do that, either. If he could actually drive. He had a feeling he could, but for some reason he didn't. Maybe he didn't have one? Strange. There seemed to be so many of them around.

* * *

On the trip home he learned surreptitiously his friend's name was Jake. Derek didn't feel like talking, but Jake was happy to keep up both ends of the conversation, rambling on and on about scoring weed, the pussy they had, how lame and awful the tiny rural town they lived in was, everything. The conversation was inane, but some thought teased him in the back of his mind. *Maybe,* some intuitive burst confided, *Jake's much smarter than this. Maybe he's keeping the patter light for a reason. But why?* Derek thought. He couldn't see a good reason to do that.

They drove into the small town. Derek imagined it looked like any other small town in existence. It was summer and hot, with sultry breezes playing through the leaves of the trees. Fields that seemed to stretch on forever, stoplights at junctions without cars waiting.

Jake slowed the car down in front of a house that looked like every other house, with the same aluminum siding that all the other houses had, and nearly the same shade of shingled roof. "Well," Jake said. "This is your stop."

Derek peered at the house. "I guess it is."

"I'll talk to you later?" Jake asked, hopefully. "Maybe tomorrow or something?"

Derek shrugged. He couldn't predict the future. But if it was up to him . . . he had no opinion either way. "Sure." He got out of the car, and headed into the house.

He pulled out some keys and tried every one until the door unlocked. He stepped in the house and looked around. It all looked familiar, but yet set apart, like he had seen it all on television. He heard noises in the other room, so he went to investigate.

An older woman was in the kitchen, logically she'd be 'mom,' but Derek decided to play it safe. He gave her a non-committal nod. She seemed surprised he was back so soon. Their conversation was brief, he managed to avoid calling her by name in the conversation. She kept sniffing the air, making a point about it. But eventually, Derek managed to excuse himself, and headed down to the basement.

He crashed for a few hours' sleep, then woke up and went to take a shower. Undressing, he sniffed the air and winced. He reeked, not just of stale beer. Maybe that's what the woman upstairs had noticed.

He stepped in the shower, letting the water cascade all around him.

* * *

The next day passed. He kept to his basement. He didn't have any real desire to get out or do anything. Or really any driving urge whatsoever.

"Derek, it's for you!" came the call from upstairs. Derek opened his eyes and scanned the room, looking for where he would put a phone. When he finally found it, he picked up.

"'Lo?" he asked into the receiver.

"Hi, ah, Derek?" the woman's voice answered.

"This is he," he replied.

"Derek, this is Mrs. Lundquist, Melanie's mother? I was

wondering . . . " she started, her voice breathy and a little asthmatic, as if talking into the phone was an effort Hercules would have had second thoughts about.

"Yeah?"

"Ah, I was wondering if you'd seen Melanie around since the camping trip? Because she, uh, she hasn't come home and I heard from Jake's mom . . . " The woman's voice drifted off.

Derek let it drift off, let there be a silence for a moment before he answered. "Nope, sorry. They drove off yesterday before Jake and I woke up. Strange they didn't show up. Maybe they're at, er . . . " He paused, trying to think of the other girl's name. But he couldn't even see either one of their faces.

"I talked to Anna's mom," the woman's voice wheezed. "Anna didn't go home either. Do you think they're at Jake's house?"

Derek said dubiously, "It's worth a shot."

"Okay . . . " The woman breathed into the phone. "I'll try there." She hung up.

* * *

Her voice, a whisper. "Y' scared? You really are?"

Pause. "I'm not scared."

"Mnh. What are you?"

* * *

A few hours later, Jake called, sounding upset. Derek told him to come over. About forty-five minutes later, Jake ended up there, knocking on the window to Derek's basement. Derek let him in, then they sprawled on the old couch.

"So, the girls have gone missing," Jake said. He bit his lip.

"Looks like it." I should say something, he thought. "Do you think we should, uh, go looking for them or something?"

"Man," Jake said, frowning. "I don't know where we would start."

"Me neither. I mean, the parks are pretty big." Derek shrugged.

"Do you remember when they left?"

"Ah, no, I . . . " Jake stopped, frowning. "I don't remember a lot of that night." He scratched his stubbly chin. "I mean, I remember the four of us hanging out together, but only in a really foggy way."

"Yeah," Derek said, "I've had a bit of memory loss myself."

"Really?" Jake asked, looking up. He looked hopeful, for some reason.

"Really. What were we doing out there, anyways? Were we just partying or something?"

Jake leaned forward, putting his elbows on his knees. "You mean the Quest."

Derek frowned. "Yeah. That."

Jake shrugged. "Well, it didn't work, obviously."

"Obviously?"

"We're still here, after all." Jake sighed, staring off to one side, his eyes unfocusing. Derek watched him, remaining still. "The funny thing is," Jake said, "I know something happened. It's not just the memory thing. We were on to something. And it's . . . thrilling, thrilling and scary at the same time, you know?"

Derek closed his eyes. He could hear the voice of the girl in his head, over and over again. He shut them tight, trying to banish the thoughts from his head. He should tell Jake, tell him everything, confess this odd amnesia. Jake was his friend, at least at some point. Before they all went off into the woods, that is. If he couldn't trust Jake, who could he trust?

"But now," Jake was rambling off, "Now I'm not sure where the girls are, I mean, what if we—"

"No," Derek said, suddenly.

Jake blinked, and looked over. "Huh?"

"No, I don't know. I don't know what you're talking about."

"What do you mean?"

"I can't remember this 'quest', or the girls, or anything."

"Holy shit," said Jake, his eyebrows both rising in concern. "You okay? I mean, maybe you hit your head at some point or something. We should get you to a hospital."

Derek shook his head. "No, I'm fine." He was. He knew it more than he knew anything else: he was fine. All was right with him, somehow. He had to trust that. He focused on Jake. "Now. What was the quest about?"

Jake blinked, looking dubious. "I can't believe you don't remember."

"I don't," Derek said, patiently. "Where did we want to go?"

"To paradise," Jake said, sadly.

* * *

What Derek remembered then, was the fury he had. The helpless rage and despair that bit and chewed at his spirit like a rabid dog. The passion made life unbearable, it was the dance on the edge of a knife: wild and unruly and dangerous, seeking to leap out of him, rend his flesh into pieces.

He was angry at the world, angry at life, angry at every little piece of rock that got stuck in his and everyone else's shoes, every irritation and pain from the most minor and trivial to the greatest of pains: the cancers of the world, the wars and holocausts of the world, the endless destruction and disease and starvation and utter hell man pressed down on one another.

Life is suffering, the Buddhists believe. That's not good enough. Life doesn't have to be suffering, life didn't need to be made harsh and cruel and awful, but it is. And people make their way through life, they live, they love, they strive for something better not because of the pain, but in spite of the pain.

And Jake, apparently, had found a way out.

* * *

He remembered driving the car down to the waters. He remembered the feeling he had within him, like he'd been leeched of emotion, of character, of being. As if someone had pricked him with a pin and it had all leaked out and bled into the seat cushions. He remembered thinking, logically, he had to do this. There was no other way.

The sunlight glinted over the waters. At one point, he would have thought it was beautiful. Now it didn't matter. Not anymore.

* * *

Someone from the Sheriff's department drove around later in the afternoon. The woman was older and a bit wider in the hips, chatted amiably with Derek's mother while holding her flat-rimmed hat in her hand.

She talked to Derek about the missing girls for a little while, but assured him the department would do what they could to find them. Derek smiled, pretending to be relieved, and a part of him felt he should be relieved that the police were looking into things. It was as if some long-forgotten rules were commanding him from distant memories, telling him, *be worried after the girls. You love them, each in their own way. . . .*

On her way out, she glanced down at Derek's arm. "Ouch, nasty scratch. Where'd you get it?"

"What, this? Oh, uh, brambles I . . . " He almost said, I think, but stopped himself. "I, you know how it is, running through bushes without really thinking about it."

"Hmm," the policewoman said, thoughtfully.

* * *

Later, on the phone with Jake. "We should find out what this ritual was. We should figure out everything we can about it. What if something happened to Melanie and Anna? They would come after us, and rightfully so."

"Oh my God," Jake said, sounding astonished. "You're right. Oh my God, what if something happened to them in the ritual? What if they're *dead*?" Panic crept into his voice.

"And what if—more likely, they're amnesiac, like you and I, but in different degrees. Maybe they're driving around as we speak, going through town after town, looking to see if one looks familiar."

There was a pregnant pause. "Yeah. Yeah, you're right. I'll come pick you up."

Derek didn't have to wait long. Jake arrived in his car, escorted him into the passenger seat, and drove off with him.

Jake lived with his parents as well, but he didn't have the luxury basement accommodations that Derek had. He lived over the garage, in a small and damp apartment. Papers were scattered everywhere, along with books of all sizes.

"I think," said Jake, "Well, you know, it's all here." He motioned vaguely to the books.

Derek glanced at him, then looked back. He picked up the books and began skimming them, looking for answers.

* * *

It seemed like hours before Jake found something that looked familiar. "Here," he said. "Read this."

Derek dropped the book he had been paging through: *Elements of Chaostrophy,* and leaned over to read the passage Jake was pointing at. It read:

> So it Be that the Almighty God hath not just his Choir of Seraphim but a Host of Angells forwhich to persue ev'ry manner of Task. & Many of which are Sente & Use & have Interest in Man. But I have known a Witche & a conjerere Who sayeth that such Angells can be Brought, or Bound, or even Tempted.
>
> Though the host of Angells are many-fold, only a few Kindes are known: Firth & Fore is the *animus viscus,* which we have spoken of the dangeres involved. For theyr Gift does not make whole, & many are misled. Also the *animus ulciscor,* a Beast of great Vengeance & a Vessle of Fury—also known as *umbra inculpatus.*
>
> But it is the *animus verita,* the Spirits of Absolution, that I Seeke. For it is said that Summoning these Beautifall beings &

petitioning to their Pitie, one can Sight the blessed realms of Heavene.

"Here," Jake said. "It looks like there's the ritual right after it."

"Can you figure it out? Figure how something might have gone wrong?"

Jake grimaced. "Maybe. What do you think might have gone wrong?"

"Anything," said Derek. "Or nothing." He looked down at the texts splayed about the room.

Jake blinked. "Or nothing?"

"Yeah," Derek said. "What if . . . what if we didn't do anything wrong. Maybe that's what happened to Melanie and Anna. Maybe they made it to this 'paradise.'"

Jake nodded. "It's . . . possible. It'd be a relief, I . . . I'm worried about them. I just feel so *stupid*, so *foolish* about all this. And I don't even know what I did."

Derek blinked. He didn't know what to say about that. He didn't feel anything about the two girls. Whatever happened to them—well, they'd manage, no doubt. "Well, look over the papers. It's our only clue."

Jake sighed. "Okay. Give me a while. How about I call you sometime tonight, after I've looked over this stuff?"

Derek shrugged. "Sure. I have nothing better to do."

* * *

At home, Derek tried to amuse himself, but nothing seemed interesting. He had a stack of games next to a console attached to a small television, but the games seemed pointless to him. His mother came down, made him do a few chores, but mostly he had the time to himself.

After a while, he decided just to lie in bed and wait. After a few hours of pointless thoughts, he drifted off to sleep.

* * *

She was a dark, shadowy figure, crouching in the underbrush with him, but it was as if there was some inner light, still, that shone her face red. He could see the veins on her face twist across it as if it was the pattern of some ancient river.

They'd gotten separated after the ritual. Melanie had run off, he sprinted through the trees to catch her. They both could hear the . . . voices up on the hill. To Derek they sounded lost, alone, panicked, confused. Insane.

"Do you think Jake and Anna are okay?" she whispered. She wobbled. She was probably as drunk as he was. Both had sobered up quickly, but their bodies were taking some time to catch up.

From what he saw, Anna was dead. With Jake, he didn't know, but it was a good bet he didn't make it. He shook his head.

"I'm scared," she said, as if allowing herself.

Derek felt the panic snaking their way through his insides with the statement. He swallowed, and Melanie turned in the shadows, her dark eyes glittering in the starlight. "Yeah," he said. He was terrified, almost enough to admit it to Melanie.

Her voice, a whisper. "Y' scared? You really are?"

Pause. "I'm not scared."

"Mnh. What are you?"

* * *

The phone rang. Derek picked it up while glancing at the clock. 12:30 AM.

"It's me," the voice said. "I think I . . . I think I've learned about all that I'm going to learn from the damn books. But I don't know where to start now."

Ah, it was Jake. He sat up in bed and thought a second, then asked. "So, what are these spirits like?"

"They're, ah, um, this kind of 'lower order' functionary, they essentially cleanse the soul in preparation for ascent into Heaven. At least, uh, that's what people *theorize* they do. I mean, this stuff's not exactly a science."

Hmm, Derek thought. "Can they kill? Are they known to kill?"

"Kill?" Jake's voice raised up an octave. "Uh, I don't *think* so. I mean, it *sounds* like it'd be out of their nature." There was a pause, Derek could hear Jake breathing on the other end. "Is . . . is there any reason why you asked that?"

"It sounds like these things are the center of our little mystery, so it's best to know as much as we can about them."

"Yeah, that makes sense." There was another long pause, then Jake asked, "Is there anything you're hiding from me?"

"No," Derek lied. "Nothing at all."

"Oh. All right. Well, what do we do now?"

"We should head up to the site and see what we can find out. That's all I can think of."

"Right, then. Tomorrow?"

"Sure," said Derek.

"Oh, and one other thing. I had a call with my dad," Jake said, his voice hinting at some kind of disgust when he uttered that three-letter word. "He said the police had contacted him, asked him a few questions. He wanted to know what the hell was up, practically ordered me to cooperate with the police, told me not to shame the family."

"Huh. It's just a missing persons thing," said Derek.

"I don't think the cops are treating it like that. I think they're treating like a murder investigation."

"Well, then. I'll see you tomorrow." He thought about it. "Better make it tomorrow morning. Early." He hung up, and fell back into bed, staring up at the empty ceiling. It had no answers. It had nothing at all.

* * *

Derek and Jake stood shivering in the woods, the ground wet and soft from the rains the night before. Even in the cool and early morning, Derek could tell it was going to be a hot, muggy day. The air clung to him like a bad relationship.

"Signs of a struggle," Derek said.

"I think we can rule 'success' out," Jake replied. His voice was tired and sad. "We're so fucked. We're so absolutely fucked."

Derek kneeled down by a stump, and ran a finger along a stained side. He smelled the brownish-red stuff collected from the stump. Blood, it smelled like rotting blood. Anna's . . . probably.

"Oh, God," Jake babbled on. "Maybe we could turn ourselves in. But what would we say? 'Sorry, but we don't remember anything.' God. God. I don't understand. They're supposed to be good spirits. *Forgiving* spirits."

Derek furrowed his brow. *They were,* he thought. *They are.* He rose up, looking at the area. If here was where Anna was standing, then Jake, who would have led the ritual, would have stood somewhere opposite of her, to the north. He stepped over the blackened pit where the bonfire was. He turned to his left. I was most likely left, he thought. To the west. Melanie to the east.

Derek stepped over to where Jake would have stood. He inspected the ground, looking for anything that looked out of place. Jake was the missing factor here—in his memory, Jake was dead or thought to be dead. But he woke up with Jake in the car. He glanced back at Jake. Maybe something had . . . happened to him in the ritual. Hmm. Derek kneeled down, then glanced to the direction where the car was. He followed it a few steps.

Leaves were unsettled, in a haphazard trail leading back to where the car would have been. Jake was dragged back to the car. Most likely by Derek. He chewed on his lip while thinking that through. Finally, he glanced back at Jake. "Learned all we needed to know?" he asked.

Jake looked pale, a little sick. "I guess so," he replied.

They headed back to the car.

* * *

"So, what do we do after this?" asked Jake as he was dropping Derek off.

"Don't know. Wait a few days, see what happens. Wait until a good idea comes up?" He shrugged.

Jake frowned, looking from Derek back down the road. He

shook his head, just slightly. "I guess we don't have a lot of options."

"No, not really."

Jake looked back. "Well, give me a call if something comes up."

"Likewise," said Derek. He got out of the car, headed to the house. He called out for his mother when he got inside, wandering the house until he found her in a little sewing room. The room looked vaguely familiar. Had it been his room at one point? Or perhaps the room of a beloved sibling? Hard to say.

"Mom," asked Derek. "Can I borrow your car?"

The older woman looked up, wrinkling her brow in concern. "Sure," she said guardedly. "But Derek, I wanted to ask you something."

"Yeah?"

"How have you been these last few weeks?" It seemed like the woman was inferring something, but Derek couldn't figure out exactly what. Apparently he wasn't that good at reading people.

"Um, I dunno. Okay, I guess."

The woman pursed her lips, just slightly. "It's just that you've seen a little withdrawn recently."

"It's nothing, Mom, really." It *was* nothing. Nothing at all. Derek didn't feel terribly withdrawn.

She rose up. "Derek, I know your brother's death has . . . " She looked away, her mouth thin and drawn, betraying tension. "It's not been easy for all of us, even after a year. But things, I mean. Things will get better. We'll be a family again."

Derek looked at her, then about the room. Beloved sibling. Ah, makes sense. "Yeah, well, can I have the keys?"

She reached in her purse and handed him the keys. "Oh, and Derek?"

"Yeah?"

"What was going on with the police people here? Is something wrong?"

He looked back at her, blinking. "Mom, you have to know by now. Melanie and Anna left our campsite and went missing."

She nodded, looking worried. Worried and mistrustful.

"I'm going back there right now. I want to look around, see if I can pick something up, find out where they went to." He shrugged again.

She nodded, seemingly about to cry. "That's the right thing to do," she said.

Derek looked at her again. He didn't know what to say to that. "Uh, thanks," he finally got out. He turned and found his way to the car.

* * *

Her voice, a whisper. "Y' scared? You really are?"

He looked back where they had run from. He could see the eerie glowing lights up there, moving around. He got them into this situation, all of them. He could get them all out again. He banished the adrenaline, tried to calm himself down. Finally, he said, "I'm not scared."

"Mnh." She was a shadow now in the darkness, but her eyes were glowing so white the irises looked dark. She sounded uncertain, suddenly. Mistrustful. "What are you?"

* * *

The rain had started again. Hot rain, drizzle, mist. Rain was meant to cool the hot climates, rain was meant to be thunder-storms, fury, the roar from the heavens followed by the gout of freezing water to set right the unbearable heat. Now the rain just added to the soupy mess of the land.

Consulting a map, he drove around the area until he found a nearby pond. It would have to be in walking distance. When he found the pond, he parked his car and walked around. He watched a blue pickup drive past.

He found where the roadway led into the pond. He wondered what happened there. Did he push the car in, then walk back? It seemed the most likely. He heard a car, glanced up to see the blue pickup drive back the other way. He stared back at the pond. A thousand tiny ripples disturbed the still surface of the waters.

The blue pickup came back. It slowed to a stop. A man called out. "Hey there, you one of the cops?"

Derek turned back. "Ah, no? I just stopped here to take a leak, check out the scenery. It's nice here."

"Yeah, nice."

Derek said, "Why'd you think I was a cop?"

"Oh, thought they started early. They're gonna dredge this old pond up."

Derek blinked. "Why?"

The man leaned out of the window a little bit, giving a conspiratorial look. He motioned to the pond. "Someone found a *hand*."

* * *

He could feel it, not just inside him, but all around him. As certain as the weight in his pocket. And he could feel, he was sure, he could feel it's own panic and confusion. He tried to concentrate, he willed himself to try. He wondered for what seemed to be the millionth time, whether this was the right thing to do.

Their bodies glowed, all four of them. Orange and red, and when he looked at the others' faces, he could see the network of dark arteries and veins across their flesh. When they opened their eyes or mouths, though, white light escaped.

"El ch'abaran," intoned Jake. "Zem-cha-na-phe."

He wondered if they had been mad to do this, until thought of Shawn, and the hatred he had for the rest of the world proved it all to him. This awful, fleshly life, with it's mortal concerns, with it's pettiness, with it's unremitting suffering, it's murder, it's constant defilement.

"Oh God," Anna cried out. "It's moving! I feel it moving inside me!"

"Relax!" Melanie hissed.

Derek looked over at Jake, tensely. Hurry up! He thought.

Jake was in a complete trance. "man-cax-mal-cas-mah," he said. "lunsemneph adao sedcatah!!"

Anna shrieked, then, and stepped forward, pretty much into the fire burning in the center. She . . . reacted to it, twisting her body, wrenching, staggering back. Derek blinked, and saw white lines start to form on her body, like rents.

Oh my God, he thought. It's trying to get out of her.

* * *

He drove back, thinking, thinking. He didn't know what he should do now. He saw no reason not to turn himself into the cops. He could sit in a cell, and sit there forever if need be. Was it the correct thing to do?

Jake. He should talk to Jake.

The time had passed when he drove up to the little garret apartment above the garage that Jake lived at. He got out and leaned against the car, looking up at the window. One light was on. He stayed there, rubbing his face, waiting and thinking.

* * *

In a flash of light, she burst apart. Derek could feel something whip past him, but he saw nothing but the bright light, heard nothing but Anna's voice extinguish and Melanie's shriek grow loud and quick. His face felt wet.

He could feel something pulling him upwards, a tug at the root of his soul. This was it, it wasn't supposed to happen this way, but still, it was happening. He wanted to collapse, leave his senses, but Melanie's screams broke his concentration.

Derek opened his eyes and looked up to see the two glowing lights, like spheres of liquid trailing light behind it, but yet amorphous, unreal. They dived and circled around one another, as if caught in each other's net.

One of them is Anna, he thought. He reached up to wipe his face, and it came off dark. The screams were trailing off, and he suddenly became frightened. Melanie. He had to get to her.

He ran.

* * *

He realized he didn't want to kill Jake. But it would be interesting, in its own way, to watch him die. And he was a participant, maybe by killing him he could learn something about what had happened, some vital clue about the Spirits of Absolution. Something that would make it all make sense.

He walked up the driveway, went around to the side, and rung the doorbell.

Jake answered. "Derek? What are you doing here?"

"I have to talk to you."

"How did you get here?"

"I drove."

"You?" Jake blinked. "You never drive. Not anymore."

"Just let me in."

Jake did.

* * *

"Y'scared? You really are?"

"I'm not scared."

"Mnh. What are you?"

She knows, he thought. No, no, there's no way. He let the question go, not answering it. Silence reigned in the dark woods. No insects or any other noises. Utter silence. He could feel the confusion of the spirits, it felt like he could hear them singing in some language that sounded so foreign and so familiar, but he didn't actually hear anything. "I have to go," he finally said. "I have to see if Jake's okay."

"Hold me," she said.

* * *

Jake was drunk. He offered Derek some whiskey, then clumsily poured him a rather large helping from his bottle. "So," Jake said. "What are you here for?"

Derek ignored the question. "I'm pretty sure Anna and Melanie are dead, Jake. And I think the cops know. I think it's only a matter of time before they figure out what happened."

Jake went pale. He nodded, and swallowed.

Derek looked up at him. Almost time. "What do you think those spirits were able to do? What were we trying to do?"

"Get . . . get a glimpse of heaven. See it for what it was. At least I think so." Jake's voice was numb, bereft of life.

"And how are they able to do that?" he goaded.

"I don't know, I don't know. I just know that they do. Why is this important?"

Derek ignored that as well. "Because," he answered himself, "they're able to pull the souls right from the body. But I wonder what would happen if the soul left the body, how the body would act?"

"I guess . . . I guess the body would collapse," said Jake, slowly. He took another heavy drink from his whiskey.

"Maybe," said Derek. "Maybe."

Jake shook his head. "I can't believe it. Anna's dead. Jesus. She was so, so beautiful, you know? Not, I mean, physically, though, though she was that too, but more just when she smiled, suddenly and honestly. I've never seen anything like that."

Derek gave him a confused look. "We were trying for our own apotheosis, all four of us. But it didn't work out the way we planned, not entirely."

Jake sighed. "You can say that again."

"Some of us didn't get to heaven, no. And some didn't get there the way they thought they would, but does the details matter? I don't know. That's for someone else to decide, not me." He looked up, "Jake, you have to die now."

Jake turned, shocked. "What?"

"You have to die, I have to kill you." Derek stood up, cracking his knuckles as if by habit.

"Why?"

"So you can join them, Jake. So your Quest can be completed."

"Jesus, Derek!" He stumbled back, holding on to the bottle in one hand. "What if I don't want to die?"

"That would make little sense."

"It's too much of a risk, Derek. I can see what you're saying, but, it's too much of a risk."

"It wasn't before, Jake."

That stopped him, at least briefly. "Yeah. Well. I've changed my priorities. I changed my mind. I have to stay here."

"What if it's your only chance, Jake? Will you regret this?"

"Maybe. But that's my fucking cross to bear. You know, Derek, you're freaking me out. I think you should leave."

Derek thought about it a moment. It would be better if he died. But he didn't want to. He balanced those two things for a moment, then realized it didn't really matter. Little did. "All right, then, you won't die, and I'll leave," he said, matter-of-factly.

Jake allowed himself to breathe. He still held the bottle like a club. He motioned to the door, then started following Derek down. "Well, what happens now?"

"I don't know. I could turn myself in, if you think that would help."

Jake blinked, looking confused again. "Uh, that's up to you."

Derek shrugged. "Fine. Talk to you later." He walked out, back to his mother's car. He drove all the way home, thinking. When he got to his house, the police cars were there.

* * *

He held Melanie close, crying in a mix of a thousand emotions: fear, anger, frustration, rage, fury, fear, fear, fear, fear, love, undying love, helplessness, hopelessness. It hadn't worked out, it was stupid, a stupid thing to do, he knew that now.

She was breathing fast against him, sniffing. Crying, probably. He could feel her heartbeat against his arms. Then he realized something.

He thought about that moment when Anna died. Just afterwards, the tug he felt, that momentary frustration. It was his soul holding on to his body. And if he hadn't been distracted, he might have gotten the apotheosis he had wished for. It was his one chance, and now it was gone. Anna had fucked it up for all four of them, and now they were stuck to clean up the mess. They wouldn't be able to cover up her disappearance. They'd be caught. They wouldn't be allowed a second chance.

They'd be stuck in even more pain and misery, until their lives gave out. They'd suffer, and suffer, and suffer, and suffer. Like Shawn suffered, but they wouldn't be taken so quickly like he was.

Melanie began now to convulse in tears, wretched sorrow. He felt her body jerk with each sob under him. With her cries, it was as if she started to glow again, bright under her skin. And he could almost feel it moving around under her skin, still.

Maybe he had a second chance. He groped down into the pocket of his jacket, grasped the handle.

* * *

The prison uniform was a bright orange, perhaps in some arcane effort to add cheer to such a drab existence. Derek waited for his mystery visitor. The guard looked bored, kept his arms folded.

He sat, as still as his body would let him, and waited.

He had signed confessions. He had repeated his story over and over again, even the lies. It had been a matter of patience for him, and patience had won out.

The door finally opened, and someone came and sat down on the other side of the partition. He recognized her immediately. "Mrs. Lundquist," he said.

Her eyes were red-rimmed. She was having trouble breathing. Even he could read the hate written loudly on the features of her face. A silver cross was prominently displayed around her neck. "Derek," she said.

He sat back and watched her. It was about the same as watching the wall.

"I wanted to see you, even though I know I shouldn't have," she started. "But I had to. You were her boyfriend, you loved her, didn't you? How could . . . " She started to cry. "How could you *do* this? Why? *Why*?" She was fighting a war against herself, a war of control. She was losing and the bitter, angry tears were going to win.

"Mrs. Lundquist," Derek began, "there is more to this existence than life."

The woman watched him, breathing for both of them. She

waited, and Derek waited with her. After a moment she said, "That's it?"

Derek nodded.

She screwed up her face. "I hope you're suffering in here," she said viciously. "And I hope you keep suffering. And when you die, I *know* you'll suffer all the more."

"No. No, I won't," he said to correct her. There was no point in lying.

* * *

He held her tightly in his arms as she sobbed, more and more helplessly, burying her face in his chest. He drew the knife and opened the blade with one hand. Mustering up his courage, shutting his eyes tightly, he jammed the blade into her back as hard as he could. She started screaming, he held on to her, his eyes shut. It's for the best, he thought. It's for the best.

"Get out of her," he growled. She responded with incoherent screams.

When he opened his eyes, the rent was deep along her back and growing. Bright light shone out from it. She had fallen to the ground, gasping. He was paralyzed then with fear and regret and worry, shocked at himself.

Then the spirits came out of her, both of them, dancing their beautiful waltz in a song he would never understand, and he felt them pulling at him, at both of them inside of him, he felt himself rising up, looking down at his body as it felt to both knees, staring up shocked and slack-jawed, and he thought, I'm free, I'm free.

Spiraling up towards the firmaments of the heavens, he took one look back at the vessel he had lived in, the one that had caused him so much pain. It was rising up, looking around at the carnage. It looked up at the sky, and he caught its expression.

There was nothing there. Nothing at all.

Printed in the United States
1397000001B/493-495

9 781930 997332